11/84   1295

Summer Of Discovery

Summer Of Discovery

Eric Wilson

Collins
Toronto

First published 1984 by
Collins Publishers
100 Lesmill Road, Don Mills, Ontario

Canadian Cataloguing in Publication Data
Wilson, Eric.
    Summer of discovery

ISBN 0-00-222633-2

I. Title.

PS8595.I4793S85 1984   jC813'.54   C84-098367-0
PZ7.W55Su 1984

Printed and bound in Canada by John Deyell Company

For Elaine Neufeld

Other books by Eric Wilson:

Murder on *The Canadian*
Vancouver Nightmare
Terror in Winnipeg
The Lost Treasure of Casa Loma
The Ghost of Lunenburg Manor
Disneyland Hostage
The Kootenay Kidnapper
Vampires of Ottawa

ONE

Ian Danoff was afraid.

As his father slowed the car, he saw a park. Two boys were tossing a ball, carefree in the summer sunshine.

Ian watched until they were out of sight, envying their freedom from fear. If only he was still at home, if only he could delay just one more day.

If only he wasn't being forced to attend camp.

"That looks like it, straight ahead."

Ian's stomach clenched. *I can't do it*, he thought. *I'm going to be sick.* Pine trees appeared, then two large stone buildings and a sign reading CAMP EASTER SEAL.

Ian's mother looked at a pool under the pines. "I hope they have lifeguards."

Ian stared at the pool. What if they forced people to swim? He wouldn't go in, not if they held a gun to him.

"We'll just get directions," Mr. Danoff said, parking the car. "Be right back, son."

Leaving him in the car, they disappeared into a stone building. A bunch of kids crossed the driveway toward the pool. Several were in wheelchairs and two on crutches. They all looked really happy. A girl stared at Ian and he dropped his eyes, feeling sad and scared.

They were all strangers and this was a horrible place. Sighing deeply, Ian looked at the nearby lake, which sparkled under the hot Saskatchewan sun.

"All set, son!" Mr. Danoff leaned in the window. "You'll love it here." He got Ian's wheelchair out and unfolded it. As he lifted Ian out of the car, Mrs. Danoff frowned. "Careful," she warned.

"I've done this a million times, sweetheart."

Mr. Danoff pushed the wheelchair toward a

ramp beside the stone building. A small bird dashed out of the sky to disappear under the eaves of the building.

"Are you nervous, son?"

"A bit."

"I can't believe this is your first time away from home. Your mother and I will miss you terribly."

"I'll be okay," Ian said quietly, wishing they'd never made him come to this horrible place. *I'm going to hate it here*, he thought desperately. *I don't want to stay!*

The building was cool inside. They entered a room with an enormous stone fireplace, a mirror along one wall, and skylights high above. There were a few other kids in wheelchairs, but most of the people seemed to be counsellors in their teens. Ian felt his fear deepen, becoming a block of ice that trickled cold water into his stomach as he was pushed toward two young women at a table.

One of them was writing on a form. The second looked up with a smile. She had blond hair, gentle eyes and light freckles across her nose. "Hi, I'm Nurse Elaine and this is Nurse Louise."

Ian looked at them doubtfully, wondering how they could be nurses when they wore T-shirts and shorts.

"Any medications?" Nurse Louise asked.

"Just Aerie-Phenom," Mrs. Danoff said, handing over a package. "It should go in the fridge right away."

Nurse Elaine wrote something on a form, then looked at Ian. "Your counsellor will be here in a minute. While you're waiting, why don't you talk to those campers?"

Ian looked at a boy and girl who stared around with scared, unhappy eyes. He was glad not to be the only camper who was afraid but he still didn't want to talk. Wheeling to a chess board, he set up some pawns and then tipped them over and looked at his reflection in the mirror. A boy with frightened eyes looked back, a boy whose hair was cut too short, a boy wearing a stupid cowboy hat, brand-new jeans, a checked shirt buttoned to the neck, and a string tie that would make anyone laugh. Yes, Ian thought unhappily, that mess is what people see when they look at Ian Danoff.

A teenage boy with curly blond hair came rushing into the room. Right away Ian knew this was his counsellor. He stared at him, envying the healthy tan, envying the relaxed way he shook hands with his parents, envying him for wearing only shorts and moccasins.

"Hi there," he said, coming over with a big grin. "My name's Parrish Tavener." He shook hands with Ian. "You're probably feeling nervous, and so am I. This is my first day as a counsellor."

Mr. Danoff smiled. "Then I wish you well. Don't make too many mistakes on our son!"

"He's very precious to us," said Mrs. Danoff, stroking Ian's hair.

"Aw, Mom." Blushing, he pushed away her hand, then felt guilty when she looked hurt.

"Let me tell you, Parrish," Mr. Danoff said, "it was a struggle to get Ian to attend camp." His voice was loud, booming around the room. Everyone was listening. "When I was a boy I attended Camp Stephens for years. Best thing that ever happened to me. It made me a man, and I'm sure this camp will do the same for Ian. He's been far too protected by us."

"He'll enjoy it here, sir."

"Just turn our boy into a man," Mr. Danoff said, then laughed heartily. "If that's not too big an order!" He knelt down beside Ian. "Well, oldtimer, it's going to be an empty house without you. Your mother and I will be lonely."

Ian nodded. His face was like a beet and his mind searched for words that would make his parents leave. "Goodbye," he finally whispered.

Mrs. Danoff bent down to kiss him. "Take good care of yourself, darling. Get lots of sleep.

Ian muttered a reply, and watched with enormous relief as his parents walked away. They paused by the door to wave goodbye, then were gone. Immediately he was overwhelmed by loneliness and longed to go with them.

Parrish put Ian's suitcase across the arms of the wheelchair. "Can you support this?"

"Of course."

"Then let's get moving!" He pushed the wheelchair into the hot sunshine. They started toward a row of cabins on a hillside. "Every kid in our cabin is new to camp this year, Ian, so you're not alone. We're going to have a ball! Isn't that right, oldtimer?"

Ian didn't answer. Instead he stared at the cabins, which were made of golden logs in a modern design. Kids sat outside playing chess. Some looked up as Ian passed along the ramp in front of the cabins, but no one said anything rude about his checked shirt.

"Here's Cabin 8!" Parrish said brightly. "Most of the guys have arrived. We're going swimming soon." Voices came through the screen door, voices of strangers. Parrish opened it.

"A new kid's arrived!" This cry came from an Indian boy, wearing a brown headband and swimming trunks. "What's your name?"

"Ian."

"Where you from?"

"Saskatoon."

"You can call me Greyeyes." The boy's thin

right arm and hand were bent up rigidly against his chest, but he grabbed Ian's suitcase with his other hand and heaved it onto a bed in a corner of the cabin. "You sleep here."

Ian looked around the large cabin. Beds stood along the log walls, the floor was linoleum with lots of open space to manoeuvre wheelchairs, and the ceiling rose to a peak.

The other boys in the room were already in their bathing suits. One of them, sitting in a wheelchair, had large black eyes and bony ribs stretching his pale skin. "Hey, kid," he said, "what goes up when the rain comes down?"

Ian shrugged, but before the thin boy could give the answer Greyeyes shouted, "An umbrella!" Then he jumped on the corner bed and bounced the springs.

A teenage girl with short brown hair who'd been putting clothes in a bureau turned around, looking annoyed. "Greyeyes, cut that out!" Then she smiled at Ian. "I'm Linda Kramer, the senior counsellor in this cabin."

"A girl counsellor?"

She grinned. "You didn't expect that, eh?"

A boy came across the cabin. Each step was a struggle. His knees almost touched, his feet were far apart and his arms swung wildly. A claw-like hand stabbed toward Ian, then the boy's neck muscles bulged with the effort of speaking. "Hi," he said, the word gurgling from deep inside his throat. "My name ... is ... Ken."

Ian sat frozen, not knowing what to do. He was frightened of this boy with the twisted limbs and strange voice, but then he saw warmth and kindness in Ken's green eyes.

Reaching forward, Ian squeezed the boy's twisted hand. "It's good to meet you," he said. Then, for the first time since arriving at camp, he smiled.

* * *

Parrish watched Ian and Ken smiling at each other, greatly relieved. Both boys seemed so quiet that it would help a lot if they became friends. The front door banged as a counsellor walked in. "Your last camper's arrived," he told Parrish.

"You kids behave yourselves," Parrish said as he left the cabin. Outside, he paused to look at the lake below. A wind made the surface choppy and blew whitecaps toward the far shore, where wild grass and trees climbed steep bluffs.

Parrish sighed as the breeze cooled the sweat on his forehead. His stomach was in knots, and a massive headache pounded behind his eyes — he was so afraid of making stupid mistakes that would cost him his new job as counsellor. Taking a deep breath, and trying to pretend the headache wasn't there, he hurried into the big stone Chalet.

"Hi," he said to a small, dark boy who waited in a wheelchair. "You my camper?"

"That's right, man." The boy flashed white teeth in a big grin. "Just call me Rico. All my friends do."

Parrish grinned. "I *know* I'm going to like you, Rico." He put the boy's suitcase across the wheelchair arms and they went outside. Feeling a surge of energy, Parrish broke into a run when they reached the ramp in front of the cabins. Rico laughed with delight as his wheelchair bounced along, then suddenly raised a warning hand. "Bump ahead, man!"

Parrish rushed forward until the last second, then stopped dead. The suitcase went flying and bounced noisily away. Rico also flew forward, but was stopped by his safety belt. He gasped for air, and then roared with laughter.

Grinning, Parrish went to pick up the suitcase. As he did, he glanced between two cabins.

Standing there was the camp director, Clay Croxley, with a face like thunder.

"Not too smart, Parrish. That boy could have been hurt."

"Sorry," he muttered, his face reddening. Slowly and carefully he pushed Rico to Cabin 8.

Inside, he noticed that Ian was the only person not changed into a bathing suit. "Hey, Ian, why aren't you ready for the pool?"

The boy looked at him with fear in his eyes. "I'm not feeling well."

"It's a bit of a stomach ache," Linda said. "I told Ian he could skip swimming today."

Parrish smiled at him. "Will you come along to the pool and be the official towel holder?"

"I guess so," Ian murmured.

"Good." Parrish opened Rico's suitcase and rummaged around, looking for his bathing suit. "Let's get you changed, kiddo."

"Hey, Rico," Norman called. "What's brown, with four legs and a trunk?"

"Beats me."

"A mouse going on vacation."

Rico laughed. "Hey, that's good. I've got to write that down."

Greyeyes watched Parrish help Rico undress, tugging his jeans down over legs that were locked tightly together. "What's wrong with you?"

"Cerebral palsy."

"What's that?"

"Search me. The doc told me once, but I forget."

Ken shuffled slowly across the room, arms swinging, and sat down on another bed. "It's ... a ... brain injury," he said, forcing the words out of his mouth. "I've got ... CP ... too."

Parrish looked at Greyeyes. "If a person's brain is injured, the messages to the muscles get all scrambled. Rico's brain keeps telling his legs to stick together."

Rico laughed. "Hey, I like that! Stick together, guys, and we won't get lost."

Some of the boys left for the pool with Linda, but Rico held up his hand before Parrish could get him out of the cabin. "Hey, man, take me back to my suitcase." Fumbling among his clothes, he found a small radio. "Can't forget this. It's got my music inside."

Everyone laughed, then headed for the pool. Ian hung back, thinking he'd rather stay in the cabin, but remembering his promise to Parrish to be official towel holder. There was something about the blond counsellor he liked, so he left the cabin to wheel along the ramp behind the others. Every face he saw, passing the other cabins, was the face of a stranger. A lump formed in his throat.

At the pool, draped in towels, Ian backed his wheelchair into a corner. He had to admit it looked like fun, the way the campers were churning up the green water, or bouncing around in the arms of counsellors. But what if there was an accident? Ian shook his head, glad he hadn't taken a chance.

A young boy came slowly toward him, a wooden cane in each hand. His sandy-coloured hair stood up in spikes, still wet from the pool. "Aren't you going in?"

Ian shook his head.

"They won't let you drown."

Ian blushed. Then, to his shame, a lie tumbled from his lips. "I've got an allergy."

"That's too bad," the little boy said, studying his eyes.

Trying to avoid the penetrating stare, Ian looked around the pool. "Hey!" he said, pointing. "Look at that guy!"

A teenager with no arms had walked to the edge of the pool and dived in fearlessly. Now he was moving swiftly through the water, his powerful legs throwing up white foam as his head bobbed above and below the surface.

"That's really something." Ian felt deeply envious of the teenager's courage. "I wonder who he is?"

"Winn Morrison. He's a C.I.T."

"What's that?"

"A Counsellor-in-Training. When I came here last year, Winn was a camper."

Ian studied Winn as he rolled and twisted through the water, as sleek as a porpoise. How did he do it? Flexing his muscles, Ian rolled his wheelchair back and forth, feeling thankful for his arms. Then he settled back to watch Winn in the pool.

A while later, to his surprise and delight, the teenager joined him. Flopping down on a bench, he grinned. "New kid on the block, huh?"

Ian smiled. There was a strength in Winn's dark eyes that made him feel safe.

"Homesick?"

Ian nodded. "I've never been away before. Pretty dumb, eh?"

"You'll love it here. I've been coming since I was little."

"This where you learned to swim?"

"Nope." Winn smiled. "I was terrified of the water until a couple of years ago. Then I was visiting a friend at her summer cabin on Long Lake. One day I walked to the end of the pier and just stepped off. I made a big splash, right where it's cold and deep."

"Why'd you do that?"

Winn shrugged. "The fear was beating me. I felt like an idiot around Sally, so I made myself learn to swim. The hard way!"

Ian joined in his laughter. He was about to admit his own fear of water when a shadow fell across his wheelchair. Looking up he saw Parrish, soaking wet from the pool.

"Got yourself a friend, Ian?" The counsellor sat down and wrapped an arm around Winn's shoulders. "This is some man. He's going to be helping us, and one other cabin."

"That's great!" Ian exclaimed.

"I'll get the other guys, Winn, so they can meet you, too."

Soon the entire group was clustered around their teenage C.I.T. "Isn't it horrible living without arms?" Norman asked. "I think I'd hate it."

Winn smiled. "It's not simple, believe me, but my foster parents never babied me. They made me cope from the start."

"Don't kids at school tease you? I get that all the time."

"Some do, but most don't. I go about my business, and people know me as just another student." He grinned. "Of course I'm handsomer than most, and brilliant, but otherwise normal."

"Were ... you," Ken said, his neck muscles bulging with the effort, "a ... camper ... here?"

Winn nodded. "I've loved every minute of it, except ..." He paused, and stared thoughtfully at the green waters of the pool. Then he shook his head. "Anyway," he exclaimed in a voice that was far too cheerful, "this is going to be the best experience of your lives!"

Ian leaned toward him. "Except what?"

"Huh?"

"You said you've loved every minute, except for something. What's that something?"

Looking confused, Winn turned to Linda. "Did I say that?"

"That's right."

"Oh. Well, anyway, it's not important."

Ian looked at Parrish. "What happened to Winn? Do you know?"

The counsellor shook his head. "Beats me."

"Come on!" Rico said to Winn. "Give us the details!"

"I shouldn't. You guys are all new to camp this summer, and I don't want to spoil it for you."

Linda shook her head. "It's too late now, Winn. They won't leave you alone until you tell."

"That's right!" Ian said. "So let's have it."

Winn sighed. "Okay, but remember this isn't my idea." He studied their faces. "Any of you believe in ghosts?"

Ian turned cold. He stared at Winn, then made himself smile. "Not me." All around him, the others nodded their agreement. Winn looked at them carefully. "Good — that makes me feel better about telling you my experience. You see, two summers ago our counsellors took us to a place that's supposed to be haunted. I didn't believe in ghosts, either, until that night."

Rico's eyes were very wide. "What happened?"

"Along the lake from here is a cluster of deserted buildings that used to be a church camp. There are some old cabins and a big place that was probably a cookhouse. There's even a tabernacle, where the kids attended church services. The whole place is abandoned. The buildings are falling apart, and wild grass grows everywhere. It's spooky when the wind blows through there."

"Why's it supposed to be haunted?"

"Our counsellors told us there was a disaster. A terrible storm blew up, taking out the power lines and knocking down trees. The camp's boats were all sunk, so they were completely cut off from civilization. The storm went on for days."

"I bet the kids loved it. I would have!"

"I think you're right, Rico. At first it probably was a lot of fun, but then it must have turned scary. Nobody knows, of course, because there were no survivors."

"What's that mean?"

"When the storm finally died down, no word came from the camp. People expected the counsellors to come into town for food but no one showed up. Finally someone phoned the Mounties, and they drove out there."

"And ...?"

"This is the horrible part. The camp was deserted. Everyone had disappeared — campers, counsellors, even the pets that used to wander around. Not a sign of life. The Mounties organized search teams, and they even brought in tracking dogs. Nothing. Finally a remembrance service was held for the kids and counsellors. The church tried to keep the camp going but no one would attend. Finally they had to shut it down and abandon the buildings. Since then they've slowly fallen to pieces."

Ian rubbed his cold arms. "That sounds impossible. People don't disappear into thin air."

"You're right, Ian. It's a strange story, and I wouldn't have believed it myself if I hadn't gone out there. It's a freaky place just to visit, but we made the mistake of convincing our counsellors to camp overnight. That's when I learned to believe in ghosts."

Greyeyes shook his head. "I don't believe a word of this, but tell us what happened."

"In the middle of the night, carried on the wind, I heard the sound of a piano. Then the voices of children singing hymns." Winn paused. "I know you don't believe me, but *I heard those voices*. So did every kid and every counsellor. At the first light of dawn we packed up and got out fast. I've never been back."

"I want to go there!" Rico exclain
to see it!"

"Me too," Greyeyes said. "That pl
great."

Ian said nothing. He just stared at
ing a tightness in his throat.

Parrish shook his head. "There's no
going there. Our activities are fully plar..ou, and
we'd need permission."

"I want to go!" Rico pleaded. He turned to
Linda. "Please, Linda. *Please!*"

She gave Winn an unhappy look. "Thanks
a lot."

He looked at the two large buildings which
dominated the camp. Their walls were made of
huge boulders, which must have taken months
to cement into place. Trees were thick everywhere, but Ian glimpsed the golden-red log cabins stretching away along the hillside. Campers
could be seen laughing and talking together, but
Ian was glad to be alone.

As his stomach rumbled from hunger, he
remembered stopping for lunch with his parents
at a highway truck-stop. If only he could be with
them now, enjoying his mother's jokes and his
father's stories about his camping days. He'd
made it sound like so much fun, but this place
looked terrible. No one would be his friend, and
the food would be worse than in hospital. At
least, when he was in hospital, his parents
visited every day.

Ian shook his head, trying to clear it of homesickness, but the feeling clung. He checked his
watch, calculating when his parents would
reach Saskatoon so he could phone and ask to be
taken home.

Then he saw the girl.

He'd seen her before, staring as he waited in
the car. Now she was coming his way in a wheel-

...r, moving swiftly. She wore a protective helmet over her dark brown hair, and had deep brown eyes. Unlike most of the girls, who were in jeans, she wore a sundress with enormous red flowers. Around her neck was a locket on a silver chain.

"My name's Susanna Wong," she said with a pretty smile.

Ian looked down at his hands, wishing the girl would leave him alone. Finally he mumbled his name.

"Feeling better? You looked pretty unhappy when you arrived at camp."

Ian shrugged.

"I was in a car accident," Susanna said. "How about you?"

"Spina bifida."

"Had many operations?"

"Six," Ian answered proudly. "Two on my feet, two on my back, and two on my head. I was hoping to make the *Guinness Book of Records*, but this year at hospital I met a girl my age who's had eighteen operations." He looked at the lake. It was so pretty, with the wind tossing whitecaps in his direction, and he smiled with pleasure. He turned to Susanna, wanting to keep the feeling alive. "What about your car accident? What happened?"

"One night, when I was seven, we were driving home from Prince Albert. A car came over a hill, on the wrong side of the road." Susanna paused, staring at the lake. "The driver was drunk," she said quietly. "He broke my back. I'll never walk again."

Ian didn't know what to say.

"I've only got one memory of the accident. I was lying on the highway, surrounded by sparkling jewels. But they weren't jewels. It was broken glass, reflecting the headlights of the cars that had stopped to help."

"Do you hate that drunk?"

"Sometimes, but the feeling makes me sick, so I try to stop."

"Ever been homesick?"

Susanna smiled. "Is that how you're feeling?"

"I guess so," Ian said, shrugging. "This is my first time away from my parents since I was born, except for being in hospital. Isn't that dumb?"

"The first time I went to school, after my accident, I was so homesick that I went into the washroom and threw up. Some of the kids were really mean, calling me names and putting sticks into the spokes of my wheelchair, but others were nice. Too nice, actually, because they did things I could have, like giving the answer to the teacher when I was still trying to work it out. Some of them even talked to me in really loud voices, thinking I couldn't understand."

Ian smiled. "I know that experience. I get it all the time, or people talk to my parents as if I'm not there. They think your head doesn't work if your legs don't. Sometimes it gets me depressed."

"I like school now, because I ignored the teasing and eventually it stopped. Then, one rainy day, I got my wheelchair stuck in the mud in the school yard. The kids all stood around watching me get soaking wet, crying my eyes out, trying to get my wheels unstuck."

Ian was shocked. "Didn't anyone try to help you?"

"Sure, but I wouldn't let them. When the bell rang the kids didn't go inside. They stood there watching while I worked the wheels back and forth. Then some teachers came out but I wouldn't let them help, either." Susanna grinned. "When I finally got the wheelchair loose there was a huge cheer from everyone. It was the best moment of my life!"

Ian smiled. "You've probably got a million friends there now."

"Not quite!"

"I tried to start a Roughriders fan club at school, so I could make some friends, but it flopped."

"What's your school?"

"It's a special one for the disabled. My parents send me there so I don't get teased."

"How rotten! Why do you let them?"

Ian shrugged. "When it comes to a struggle, my parents know every trick in the book. My mom cries, and Dad says *we know best* in his loud voice. I don't know how to stand up for myself." He paused, then sighed. "I didn't want to come to this camp, Susanna. It was their idea."

"I'm sorry. I should never have mentioned it."

"It's too late now." She turned to the boys. "Okay, I'll speak to the camp director about getting the bus. Maybe we can go tomorrow for a couple of hours."

"I want to camp overnight!" Greyeyes begged. "Please, Linda."

"Absolutely no way." She held up her hand. "No more arguments, no more pleading. Two hours at the ghost camp is all you get."

"That's better than nothing!" Rico said. "Three cheers for Linda."

All the boys joined the cheer — except Ian.

His mouth was too dry.

TWO

Wanting to be alone, Ian left the pool to wheel down to the lake. Burned in his mind was the image of the ghost camp with the wind blowing through the old buildings and children's hymns carried on the wind. He shivered, wishing Winn had never mentioned it.

In the distance, a storm was crossing the prairie. Thick streaks of black rain slanted down from the clouds, and lightning flicked to the earth. Thunder grumbled inside the storm, making a sound like giant bowling balls crashing together.

A cool breeze ruffled Ian's shirt. Above his head, a flag fluttered high on a pole. Ian's fingers went to the side of his wheelchair, where he'd put a decal of the Canadian flag, but touching it today didn't bring him comfort. He was too scared.

"Listen!" she whispered, putting a warning hand on Ian's arm, then pointing at the long green grass. Rustling and quivering, it suddenly parted as a small field mouse appeared. Its tiny eyes darting about, the mouse briskly munched some food before disappearing.

"Was that a mouseburger he was eating?"

Susanna laughed. "You only think of your stomach," she said, wagging a finger in his face. "I'd better take you in hand."

Ian blushed. "Susanna, it's good talking to you. I've told you all the secrets of my life."

"I bet there's more."

"Maybe," Ian said, then saw Parrish coming their way. "That's my counsellor. I wonder what he wants?"

"He's so cute, I hope he wants to meet me."

Ian laughed. "I'll introduce you."

As Parrish chatted to Susanna, Ian studied

his blond hair and blue eyes. He couldn't help envying the counsellor's good looks, and his relaxed conversation. Here was someone without a care in the world. *How nice that would be,* Ian thought as his homesickness came flooding back.

Minutes later Ian cheered up again when he started a tour of the camp with Parrish and they entered the Craft House. Paint, leather, beads, all kinds of material lay waiting. "I love this kind of stuff!" Ian exclaimed. "I didn't think we'd be making things here."

"Our first crafts session is tomorrow."

"I'd like to carve one of those." Ian pointed at a tall totem pole on display. "Would you teach me how?"

"No, but I'm sure the crafts counsellor will. When it comes to making things I'm all thumbs. My grandmother still has a table I made in grade seven. It's got the wobblies."

"I think I'll make my grandparents one of those ceramic candy dishes."

They returned to the sunshine. The warm light poured through the pines to light up the two huge stone buildings. "This place started out as a luxury hotel," Parrish said. "It was built during the Depression by unemployed workers, then later converted into Camp Easter Seal."

"Do any adults come here?"

"Sure thing. After you guys leave there'll be a Double Disabled session. It's for adults who are both physically and mentally handicapped. I guess about 600 people will camp here this summer, and with luck I'll meet a lot of them."

"With luck? What do you mean?"

"I'm on probation, Ian. I was given this job only a few days ago, because another counsellor was fired. Since I didn't have a full training session, my performance will be watched by the

Director. If I do a poor job with you guys, I lose my job."

"What would happen then?"

"I'm not sure." Parrish grabbed the handles of Ian's chair and started pushing him up the hill in the direction of the cabins. "There are other possibilities, but I want to stay here."

"How come? I want to go home."

Parrish laughed. "You'll feel different in a day or two. We'll get you into that pool, and out on horseback, and you'll feel great."

"Horseback? There's riding here?"

"Yup. Good news, eh?"

"Sure," Ian said quietly. He remembered his parents taking him on holiday to Alberta. At a ranch, his father had made a mistake and pushed his wheelchair too close to some horses. Hooves had lashed out against the chair, knocking him into the dust. Sometimes, in his nightmares, the hooves still flew at him. "Do we get to choose our activities here?"

"What do you mean?"

"Well, for example, could I take extra crafts and skip the riding?"

Parrish didn't answer until they reached a grassy patch near the cabins. Then he set the wheelchair brakes and sat down beside Ian. He snapped off a stalk of long grass, put it in his mouth, leaned back on one elbow, and finally spoke.

"Are you afraid of horses, Ian?"

"I, uh ..."

"And what about the pool? Did you really have a stomach ache, or was it a bad case of nerves?"

Ian felt his face turning red. He reached for a stalk of grass, jammed it into his mouth, and looked out over the lake. Gulls soared over the whitecaps, free and happy in the wind.

"Well, Ian? You can tell me."

"You see, I ..."

"I'll take you riding, Ian. I'll be on the horse, sitting behind you. I won't let you fall off."

"It's not that ..."

"Ian, let me say something." Parrish reached for another stalk. "When I was a kid, younger than you, I wanted to play baseball so bad I could taste it. But every time I stepped to the plate I was shaking with fear. I kept thinking the ball would hit me in the face. I was the easiest strike-out on the team until we had a practice and the coach forced me to stand at the plate while he threw baseballs past me. First he threw them wide, then closer and closer. Eventually they were just missing me, but by then I'd lost my fear. I became a dynamite batter, and people say I should go for the majors."

"That coach sounds stupid. What if he'd hit you?"

"That's not the point, Ian! He forced me to face my demons, and beat them down." Parrish leaned forward, his blue eyes bright. "I want to do the same for you, Ian. Let me show you there's nothing to fear *except the fear.*"

Ian looked at his hands. He pictured his parents driving to Saskatoon, laughing and talking. No one had trapped them at Camp Easter Seal with a fanatical counsellor.

"Well, Ian?"

"I'm not sure ..."

"Let's go to the pool right now and jump in, clothes and all. It'll be a real laugh, and you'll see there's nothing to be afraid of."

"But this outfit cost my parents a lot of money! They got it new for my trip to camp."

"Your clothes will dry." Parrish jumped up, slapping his hands together. "This is going to be great, Ian. Let's go for it!"

Ian grabbed the brakes of his chair, and held

on tight. "I don't want to, Parrish. My parents will be furious if my clothes get wrecked."

The counsellor looked at him thoughtfully. "Okay," he said at last. "Then how about it if I show you more of the camp?"

"Okay. I guess so."

They went together along the row of cedar-log cabins, their faces brushed by the wind which came off the prairie beyond the cabins. The leaves of the poplars rustled above their heads, giving Ian a peaceful feeling. Then the home-sickness came creeping back as they stopped to watch a chess match and the kids looked at him with eyes that seemed suspicious and unfriendly. He wondered if they were also feeling lonely, but he doubted it.

Parrish introduced himself and Ian to the boys, who were both in wheelchairs. "We're in Cabin 8. How about if we challenge you guys to a chess tournament?"

"All right," one of the boys said quietly. "I like chess."

Parrish looked at Ian. "Do you play?"

"Sure."

"Figure you can take this guy?" Parrish gave the other boy's shoulder a friendly squeeze. "He's pretty good. Two more moves and his rook will have the king in check."

"Hey!" the boy exclaimed. "Don't give away my strategy."

Parrish laughed. "We'd better leave you alone."

Once again, Ian found himself envying Parrish's easy manner, wishing he didn't feel so awkward around people. He wasn't used to strangers.

"Got any brothers or sisters?" Parrish asked, as they turned in the direction of the big stone chalets.

"No."

"Tell me about your friends."

"I guess I don't have any. Not what you'd call real friends. Some kids at school I talk to."

"I'm surprised, Ian. Friends make life fun. I'd be really lonely without the people I care for."

"I don't understand how to make friends. I never know the words to say."

"Well, maybe you'll find some at camp."

"Maybe," Ian mumbled. "I hope so."

"How do you feel about being in that chair?"

"I'm used to it, so usually it's okay. Sometimes I get sick of looking up at people all the time. It makes my neck sore."

"Do you talk to your parents about your feelings?"

"All the time. They're so nice to me, you wouldn't believe it." The image of his parents' smiling faces loomed in front of Ian. "I wish ..."

"Yes?"

"I wish I hadn't pushed my mom's hand away. She must feel terrible."

"I'm sure she's completely forgotten it, Ian. Right now she'll be concentrating on you, hoping things are good at camp and you're happy."

"You think so?"

"I know so." They moved to one side of the ramp as a boy with leg-braces approached. He was dressed entirely in cowboy gear, and raised his Stetson in greeting. "Hiya, Tex," Parrish said, giving the boy a friendly poke as he went by. "So, Ian, are you happy?"

"I guess so, Parrish. It's nice talking to you."

As they passed the back of the dining hall, which was one of the stone chalets, a screen door opened. Out came a counsellor wearing a T-shirt and shorts. Vivid red hair was swept back from her face and hung to her waist; her eyes were blue, and she gave Ian a nice smile before looking at Parrish.

"Hi!" she said. "Do you remember meeting me when you first arrived here? My name's Dani Darin."

"Sure, Dani, I remember you." A blush appeared beneath Parrish's tan. "This is Ian Danoff. He's new to camp, too, so we're having a look around."

"May I join you?"

"Sure thing."

At first Ian was pleased to have Dani's company but then he began to feel left out. Although the two counsellors directed a few comments his way, they spent most of their time talking to each other while Ian wheeled along feeling lonely. After going to the lakeshore, where they watched a game of horseshoes, Dani suggested looking at the farm.

"It's actually just a few chickens and goats," she said, laughing, "but everyone calls it the farm. It's near the caretaker's house, just a few minutes from here."

The animals were inside a large pen, behind a wire fence. The goats were nowhere in sight, but a few chickens strutted around while a rooster perched at the top of a wooden shack.

"We should have brought them something to eat," Ian said, then smiled at Dani. "But I'm not sure what chickens eat. I've always lived in the city."

"I'm a country girl myself. Born and raised on the farm."

"What's that like?"

"Fun, and lots of hard work. My parents have us up early every day doing the chores. But the food is delicious, and I've got lots of pets."

"I'd love to visit your farm."

"Come any time, Ian." She glanced at Parrish. "You too, if you'd like."

He smiled. "Thanks, Dani."

"What kind of pets do you have?" Ian asked.

"My favourite is Bossy. She's my cow. Her ears are the softest velvet you've ever touched."

"Does she ever kick? I've heard cows do that, when they're being milked."

Dani shook her head. As she did, Parrish glanced at Ian. "Ever held a chicken?"

"No."

"Like to try?"

Ian flicked his eyes toward Dani, then looked down at his hands. He felt his skin turning red. "I'm not sure. Maybe tomorrow would be a good time."

Parrish unhooked a strand of wire that held the gate in place. As he entered the pen, chickens scattered in every direction with wings flapping. The rooster raised himself angrily, but Parrish ignored all the commotion as he managed to trap a chicken in a corner of the pen.

Ian's heart was thumping as Parrish approached with the chicken. It was squawking angrily and its bright eyes stared fiercely at the counsellor, who was grinning in triumph. "This one's got some spirit! Come on, Ian, hold out your hands."

"I ..." Ian stared at the chicken's powerful beak. "Maybe ..."

Dani reached for the chicken. "Let me have it." Kneeling down beside Ian's wheelchair, she looked at him. "Just stroke the feathers on its back, Ian." When he had touched the feathers, which were dry and coarse, she tossed the chicken back into the pen and closed the gate.

"I'd better get back to my campers."

Parrish smiled at her. "We enjoyed your company. See you again, Dani."

"I hope so. It was nice talking to both of you. You're going to love camp, Ian."

He couldn't look at her. Instead he stared at

the chickens inside the pen. They seemed so small from a distance, but up close that beak had looked like it would draw blood. His face flushed as he thought about revealing his fear to Dani.

From the distance came the loud clanging of a bell. "Supper time!" Parrish said. "Are you feeling hungry?"

"I'm not sure."

"Well, let's go see what they're serving."

Minutes later they crossed a paved patio between the two chalets, and entered the dining hall. It was cool inside, with a high ceiling. There were about twenty long wooden tables set with cutlery and plastic cups, and large bowls filled with spaghetti and salad awaited the campers. The air was loud with noise as people called to each other, sorting out where each group of campers would sit.

"I don't want any supper," Ian said, feeling lonely as he stared at all the strangers. "I'd rather lie down in the cabin."

"Nonsense!" Parrish's voice was sharp. "Have some food and then you'll feel better." Before Ian could reply, he pushed him toward a nearby table where Linda and the other boys were waiting. They also looked lonely and he remembered Parrish saying everyone in the cabin except Linda was new to camp.

He manoeuvred his wheelchair into a space beside Norman, the thin boy who'd been cracking the terrible jokes. "How are you doing?" he asked, feeling shy.

Norman turned to stare at him. His glasses were very thick. "Hey, kid, are you a PLP?"

"I'm not sure what you mean."

"I bet you are a Public Leaning Post." He leaned against Ian, digging a sharp elbow into his ribs, then crowed with laughter. "Hey, Rico, are you a PLP?"

"No way, man!"

"You're not a Proper Looking Person? Too bad!"

As Norman roared with laughter, Ian looked at Rico. "This guy's jokes are terrible. We should call him Corny."

"Good thinking."

Parrish shook his head. "No nicknames."

"Why not?"

"I'm not sure, but it doesn't seem fair."

Norman grinned at Parrish. "I don't care what they call me, as long as they call me first to eat." He looked at Greyeyes, the Indian boy who wore a brown headband. "Hey, kid, how does a tailor make trousers last?"

"How would I know, Corny?"

"He makes the coat first." He made a noise like a rooster, then laughed so hard he almost choked. "Hey kid, boo."

Greyeyes made a face. "What?"

"It's a knock-knock joke. You're supposed to say boo, who."

"Okay," Greyeyes said impatiently. "Boo, who?"

"No need to cry about it."

As Corny pounded the table, delighted with his wit, Ian saw Susanna coming his way in her wheelchair. Immediately he felt better, especially when she joined him at the table. With her was a teenage girl who had sunburnt skin, long hair the colour of snow, and eyes with pink pupils. Sitting down beside Ian, she smiled in his direction.

"My name's Mary, but everyone calls me Speedball."

As Ian introduced himself, he realized the counsellor was blind.

"I've got some vision," Speedball said, as if she could read his mind. "About five percent, but

I'm legally blind. Which doesn't mean Susanna and the other kids in my cabin will get away with anything!"

"Where'd you get your nickname?"

Before she could answer, Susanna leaned forward. "Speedball was my counsellor last year, too. She's a fantastic track star. Last summer she went to the Olympiad for the Disabled, and won four golds. When she came home, she got to meet the Premier. I saw her on TV!"

Another camper pointed across the dining hall at a teenager with bushy hair. "That guy holds a world record. He did 1.86 metres in the high jump."

"Are you sure that's a world record? People have jumped higher than that."

"Sure, but not with one leg!"

"Wow!" Ian took a closer look at the teenager, then shook his head. It was interesting to be surrounded by champions, but it was also pretty depressing. He looked down at his plate, feeling glum.

Parrish watched Ian from the other end of the table, wondering how to get the sadness off his face. When he'd first gone to camp, as a little kid, he'd had a great time from the moment he arrived. He remembered his counsellor giving him a special award as "the funniest kid in camp." Now he'd grown up and become a counsellor himself, but he didn't know how to deal with a camper who was both homesick and afraid of life.

Sighing, Parrish looked at Ken. The boy's cheeks and chin were bright with spaghetti sauce. More food splattered onto the table as he raised another forkful with his shaking hand, but a look of great happiness was on his face. Chatting to him was Winn, who'd leaned his chair against the wall and was holding a fork and spoon with his toes. With great dexterity, Winn twirled the strands of spaghetti before lifting the food to this mouth.

Parrish looked again at Ken, wondering how it felt to be trapped inside a body that was your enemy. Ken's brain signalled *lift the fork* but instead the muscles made his arm shoot straight out, or fly into the air. *Stand up straight*, said Ken's brain, but the muscles coiled into hard knots. *Talk to this nice girl*, but the words refused to come.

Parrish turned to a girl in a wheelchair beside him. She was very tiny, with her body curled in a tight ball. Spaghetti sauce stained her lips. "What's your name?"

"Tracy." Her voice was barely a whisper.

"I hope you chew each mouthful thirty-six times. That's what my grandmother tells me to do."

She grinned.

"Miss your folks, Tracy?"

"I don't have a family."

"Where do you live?" Parrish asked, leaning close to hear.

"In a rehabilitation institution."

"What's that like?"

"Not bad," Tracy said, then smiled, "but the attendants aren't great-looking guys like you. I wish you worked there. You could give me backrubs."

"Boy, what a line!" Parrish laughed. "I bet the attendants love you."

The smile left the girl's tiny face. "They don't care about any of us. After we've finished on the toilet, we're supposed to ring a handbell and somebody's supposed to come and get us. I can hardly lift the bell, it's so big. One day I rang it for a half-hour and they just ignored me. I could hear them standing outside the door, talking to each other."

"So what happened?"

"I threw the bell on the floor. They still didn't come."

Parrish reached for her hand. The fingers closed around his like talons of a small bird. He had to swallow hard, and fight down his outrage that people could treat other people this way, but then he looked down at the girl's smiling face. Looking around the dining hall, at the happiness on other faces, he suddenly realized the importance of a large banner which read:

> We're so glad you're here.
> It makes us realize
> just how beautiful
> our world is.

* * *

When supper was over, Ian sat by himself on the patio between the stone buildings, watching little birds at play in nearby bushes and trees. As he smiled, watching a brown sparrow take a dust bath, he realized his homesickness was fading.

The loud *clang-clang-clang-clang* of the camp bell startled him, then other people started leaving the patio. What was going on? He began to feel lonely as counsellors pushed other campers away in their wheelchairs, while he sat alone and unnoticed. At last a man with a black beard came out of the Chalet.

"Who's your counsellor?"

"A guy named Parrish."

"Where is he?" the man asked, frowning.

Ian shrugged.

Linda came running around a corner of the

Chalet. "Sorry, Clay," she said to the man, then pushed Ian's wheelchair across the patio.

"Who was he?"

"Clay Croxley. He's in charge of the camp."

"Where are we going?"

"Campfire."

They followed a winding road to a trail that ran parallel to the lakeshore. As they did, the sweet sound of singing was carried on the evening air:

> Fire's burning, fire's burning
> Draw nearer, draw nearer,
> In the glowing, in the glowing,
> Come sing and be merry.

After jouncing over rocks and half-buried roots, they entered a clearing surrounded by poplars and tall pines. Orange-red flames leapt from a campfire. A circle of campers was staring at the shifting patterns of flame that cut the dark shadows of the clearing.

A girl wearing a purple-patterned blouse and old jeans tossed a few twisted chunks of wood into the fire. She watched the flames eat hungrily into the dry bark, then led the singing of a calypso that required elaborate hand-and-arm motions. Ian noticed a young girl shaking a leather strap that held several jingle bells. The girl, who was blind and had a large hearing aid in each ear, was singing in a loud and off-key voice. Ian smiled, despite his homesickness, and decided to join in the song.

"Marshmallow time!" the teenage girl announced after a few more numbers. Ian didn't like the taste of marshmallows, so he wheeled close to Winn. "Wow, you're great with those feet," he said, watching him spear three of the spongy white blobs onto a branch, then thrust it close to the flames. As the marshmallows were transformed into a golden brown, Winn licked his lips in hungry anticipation.

A small flame suddenly appeared on the marshmallows. "Hey!" Winn shouted in dismay, watching his marshmallows turn black. When he touched one to his lips, the black shell collapsed and he was left with a bit of white goo clinging to the branch.

"Tough luck," Ian said, grinning. Then he saw Susanna waving, and went to join her and the other girls in her cabin. They were so friendly that he soon found, to his surprise, that he was telling them a story about some troubles his mother had with marshmallows on a cookout. To his pleasure, the girls laughed so hard that tears rolled down their faces.

"You sure can tell a story," Susanna said, wiping her face.

"You bet," whispered Tracy, the tiny girl whose body was in a tight ball. "Got another one?"

This time Ian treated them to an account of the day his father discovered, when he was half way across a field, that he was sharing the space with a large, unfriendly bull. This story was also a hit, and Ian was just about to launch into another when Susanna held up her hand.

"I'll hear this another time, Ian. Campfire's almost over, and I haven't had a chance to talk to Parrish." Susanna eyed him across the campfire flames.

Tracy smiled. "We were holding hands."

"Lucky you! He can hold my hand any day."

At that moment, Parrish looked at her and smiled. "Wow!" Susanna whispered, "look at those eyes!" As Parrish came over to chat with her and Tracy, Ian felt jealous. Finally, he couldn't stand it any more.

"Do you believe in ghosts?" he asked Tracy.

"Are you crazy? Of course not."

"Neither do I, but Winn says there's ghosts nearby. Along the lake, where a church camp used to be."

"He's putting you on."

"Probably, but our cabin's going there tomorrow to investigate."

"Parrish!" the girl exclaimed. "I want to visit the ghost camp."

"It's probably nothing special," the counsellor said, but within minutes he'd agreed to find out if the girls' cabin could go on tomorrow's trip.

"Form a circle!" someone called.

Ken shuffled across the clearing to be at Ian's side while, all around the fire, people joined hands. Everyone was silent, watching the red embers. One voice began to sing quietly, then was joined by the rest:

> Day is done, gone the sun,
> From the lake, from the hills,
>   from the sky.
> All is well, safely rest,
> God is nigh.

The song was beautiful. Ian felt a soft glow of pleasure as the circle rocked gently back and forth, united. The man with the black beard stepped forward.

"I'm Clay Croxley, the Camp Director. It's good to greet old friends, and welcome new faces. I think we'll all make many discoveries at Camp Easter Seal that will make us richer people. Good luck, and happy camping."

Returning to his place between Rico and a girl, Clay led the circle into the final song:

> Friends, friends, friends

We will always be;
Whether in fair
Or in dark stormy weather,
Camp Easter Seal
Will keep us together.

The song ended, there was a moment of quiet, then the clearing was rocked by a loud shout from dozens of throats, "Thanks for the evening, campers!" Even though he knew it couldn't last, Ian was sad that the spell was broken.

He thought of his parents, safely home by now. There was still time to phone. By this time tomorrow he could be back in his own bedroom, working on his model of a Stutz Bearcat.

Parrish came to kneel beside him. "How are you feeling?" he said gently. "Missing your parents?"

Ian nodded. The sympathy in the counsellor's voice made tears rise inside his eyes.

Parrish squeezed his hand. "Try to get through until tomorrow, Ian. Then, if you're still feeling blue, I'll arrange for you to phone them."

"Thanks," Ian whispered.

"Think you can manage?"

"I guess so. Will you be sleeping at the cabin, too?"

"Sure thing, oldtimer. Now let's get to the biffy for a wash behind the ears before you hit the sack."

The biffy was a large cedar-log building with a row of sinks along one wall, some toilets and a couple of bathtubs. Lights burned from the ceiling throwing a cold light on Ian as he wheeled to a sink. Blobs of old toothpaste were stuck to the enamel, and a long hair was attached to some soap left behind by another camper. "Gross," Ian whispered to himself. The sparkling bathroom of his home seemed a distant memory.

He brushed his teeth quickly, splashed a bit of water on his face, then rubbed it with a towel. He felt weary, but he wasn't looking forward to sleeping in a strange bed in a strange place with a bunch of strangers snoring all around.

Linda and Parrish were giving backrubs when he returned to the cabin. Rico had a big smile on his face as Parrish kneaded the muscles of his back, and Corny seemed happy as he produced his hundredth joke of the evening, but both Ken and Greyeyes lay on their beds looking sad. Ian wanted to say they weren't alone in their blues, but instead he rolled to his own bed. Lifting himself out of the wheelchair on strong wrists, he got onto the bed and heaved his legs inside the sleeping bag.

A few minutes later, Parrish gave him a vigorous backrub while telling jokes that were worse than Corny's. After the nurses had visited to check each camper's health, Linda hung some old blankets across her corner of the cabin for privacy and said good night. Winn left for the Chalet, where the C.I.T.'s slept, and Parrish switched out the lights before going to his bed.

Ian lay with his hands behind his head, looking at the yellow glow coming through the screen door from the porch light. In Saskatoon he had no trouble falling asleep because he knew every sound the house made, but this cabin creaked under the wind and tree branches tapped against the roof. Ian looked at the glowing dial of his watch. His parents would be watching the local news on TV and drinking hot chocolate. Maybe they'd also be thinking of him.

The screen door opened, and the dark shape of a man entered the cabin. Ian's heart lurched, then he recognized Clay Croxley. The Director walked around the cabin checking each camper before leaving quietly.

A long time passed but Ian was unable to fall asleep. Finally, in desperation, he tried counting sheep but even that didn't work. He gave himself up to a night without sleep.

Then a strange thing happened.

Parrish threw back his blanket and got out of bed. Ian was surprised to see the counsellor was still wearing jeans and a shirt. He pulled on some shoes, then went to the door and stood looking out.

For a long time he remained there, occasionally sighing. Then he pushed open the door and stepped outside. After being visible for a moment under the yellow porch light, Parrish was gone.

Quickly Ian got into his chair and wheeled across the cabin. Shading his eyes against the glare of the porch light, he looked into the night. Silent explosions of lightning came from a distant storm, filling the sky with their white light and showing the outlines of low trees and bushes.

They also showed the outline of Parrish, running swiftly away from camp.

THREE

Ian was in a dark room. He tried to find a door to freedom, but his eyes were blind. Hot tears ran down his cheeks.

A sudden white light exploded. His eyes flew open and he saw the cabin filled with brilliance. His wheelchair was beside the bed, beyond it the shape of Greyeyes asleep under tangled blankets.

Just as Ian's tingling nerves began to relax, there was a BANG. Rain splattered down on the roof. Another burst of lightning was followed by a roll of thunder that went on and on, crashing and banging as it died away into the distance.

Ian remembered Parrish running into the night. The counsellor had been gone for more than two hours before finally creeping back into the cabin, groaning with weariness, to fall into his bed.

What was Parrish's secret?

Ian tried to puzzle out the answer, but his eyes were heavy and soon he slept again. Nothing more disturbed him until he heard a trumpet, followed by a voice crying, "Hear ye! Hear ye! Rise and shine!" Clay Croxley stood in the cabin, grinning as he made the trumpet blare. Stretching his arms, Ian looked at Parrish's sleeping figure. Where had he gone last night?

"Hey, Linda." It was Corny, back in action with his jokes. "Why does a giraffe have such a long neck?"

Linda's sleepy voice came faintly from her bed. "I give up."

"To attach its head to its body."

Rico laughed, but everyone else was silent. At last there was movement from Ken's direction as the boy worked his way into a sitting position. With a tremendous effort, he was able to get a

T-shirt over his head, then struggled until finally he'd got it on.

Ian glanced at his watch. It had taken Ken ten minutes to put on the T-shirt. Sitting up, he got dressed with lightning speed, then swung into his wheelchair. Rolling across the cabin, he stopped by Ken. The boy had one leg into his jeans, but the other was refusing to cooperate. Sweat shone on Ken's face, and there was anger in his green eyes as his legs jerked and thrashed.

"Want some help?"

For a moment there was silence, then a single word rose from deep inside Ken, "No!"

Blushing, Ian turned away.

Within minutes Linda was out of bed, and Winn had arrived to help the campers get ready. But Parrish remained asleep, snoring loudly. Finally, as the distant bell announced breakfast, Greyeyes tipped a cup of water over his face.

As the counsellor sat straight up, shocked, Greyeyes ran from the cabin laughing gleefully. Parrish dragged himself out of bed and managed to get to breakfast, but his eyes were still full of sleep when they returned for clean-up. As he pushed a broom around the cabin, his mouth produced huge and noisy yawns.

Ian straightened the sleeping bag on his bed, then sat back in his wheelchair. The others had all found jobs to do — Greyeyes was even cleaning the windows — but he'd never done housework before and wasn't in the mood to learn how.

"Come on, Ian!" Linda called across the cabin. "Grab a cloth and do some dusting."

"That's not a man's job!"

She laughed. "Time's have changed, buddy. Get to it, or we'll never win the cabin-inspection award."

Using the cloth she threw his way, Ian pushed

around some of the dust on his bedside table. Then he reached inside for his copy of *Terry Fox: His Story* and looked at some of the photographs. "You know something? We should give our cabin a name."

Rico looked up from making his bed. "Good thinking."

"What . . . name?" Ken asked. "Ghost kids . . . hang . . . out?"

"That's pretty good," Ian said, "but how about calling it Terry Fox Cabin?"

"I . . . like that!"

"Me, too," Greyeyes said. "Terry Fox was a great runner, just like me. But I doubt if I could run half-way across Canada with an artificial leg."

"You're a runner?"

"Sure. My coach says I'm a natural. If I did more training, she says, I could reach the top."

Ian looked at Greyeye's withered arm, held tight against his chest. "What about your disability?"

Greyeyes hooted. "I don't run on my arms, you jerk!"

For a moment Ian's feelings were hurt, then he laughed. There was something about Greyeyes that he liked. "I guess you're right, but I could almost win a race on *my* arms." Swinging easily out of his wheelchair, he dropped to the floor. Then, with amazing speed, he scuttled backwards across the cabin, propelling his body with his arms.

Reaching the wall, Ian made a fast turn and came flying back, moving even faster. When the others broke into applause, he raised his fist in a victory salute. "Too bad that's not an Olympic event!"

Rico laughed. "Where'd you get those muscles, man?"

"I pump iron at home, and do the Canada Fitness Awards at school. I want to get a Panther, one of those special stripped-down chairs for racing, but you know what? My folks want to spend the money on a power wheelchair."

Parrish looked at him. "How do you feel about that?"

"Not too good. It's like they're trying to turn me into a wimp run by electricity."

"Why not tell them so?"

Ian shrugged. "You don't know my folks. Their word is law."

Corny nodded. "I know what you're saying. My big ambition is to get a pilot's licence, but Dad says it's impossible."

Parrish shook his head. "Nothing's impossible, Corny. Why does he say that?"

"Because I'm in this wheelchair."

"But a pilot doesn't use pedals to get a plane into the air."

Corny laughed, but there was sadness in his eyes. "Tell that to my dad."

Linda sat on the bed beside him. "Every summer a group called the Flying Farmers take campers up for a ride. It's unfortunate they won't be coming while you guys are here or you could have met Otis Blackwood. He's a paraplegic, paralyzed from the waist down, but he flies his own plane with hand controls he designed."

Corny sighed. "My dad should talk to you and Parrish."

"Get him on the phone," Parrish said. "I'll set him straight." Then he looked at Ian. "What about you, oldtimer? Still want me to phone your parents, or is the homesickness gone?"

Ian blushed. "It's gone," he mumbled, then glanced at the others. No one seemed to have noticed Parrish's comment. "What a dream I had last night! A motorcycle gang attacked the camp but all us guys fought them. You know what finally saved us?"

"I know!" Greyeyes said. "They finally got a close look at your face."

"Nope. Corny started cracking jokes, and the gang fled in terror."

Everyone but Corny laughed. "My jokes are excellent," he protested.

"You're right," Ian agreed, "and I think you should be on the stage. There's one leaving in an hour."

Parrish shook his head. "That's enough, Ian. No need to get nasty."

Ian dropped his eyes. "Sorry."

"Hey, Linda," Rico said, "when do we actually *do* something around this camp?"

"Right after cabin inspection we head for archery. Meantime, who wants a game of chess?"

Rico accepted the challenge, and Corny wheeled over to watch. Greyeyes and Parrish lay down on their beds, while Ian searched his bedside table for his journal. It was his ambition to be a writer, so he got to work on a long account of his first hours at Camp Easter Seal. He couldn't describe his homesickness, which had faded like the memory of being ill fades, but a pulse beat in his throat when he thought about the ghost camp. *Crazy to be so nervous*, he wrote, *but I feel something terrible is going to happen there.*

Looking up from his journal, Ian saw Ken taking a deck of cards out of his bedside table.

Cards?

Ian watched the boy's efforts to control his shaking hands as he removed the cards from their package. This was successful, but then he suddenly lost control. The cards scattered across the floor.

Parrish rolled off his bed to kneel beside Ken. "I'll give you a hand, good buddy."

"Please ... don't."

"What?"

"I ... made ... the mess." Ken paused for breath, then forced out more words. "So I ... clean ... it up."

"That's great, Ken, but there are fifty-two cards in the deck. It'll take you a long time. Please let me help."

"I want ... to ... do it ... myself."

Parrish studied Ken's green eyes. "How about if we share the job?" Quickly he swept most of the cards into a pile. He picked up all but two, which remained on the floor. "You get those, Ken."

But the boy went to his bed.

"Hey! Aren't you going to help?"

"Do you ... think ... I'm ... useless?"

"Of course not, Ken. I just don't want you to miss archery."

"Picking up ... the cards ... was ... more important."

Parrish looked down at the cards in his hand. Clearly he was trying to decide if he should scatter all the cards again and let Ken pick them up.

Finally he walked over to Ken, and held out his hand. "I'm sorry," he said quietly. "I didn't understand."

Ken's mouth twisted in a smile, then his hand stabbed toward Parrish's. "It's ... okay. Just don't ... feel ... sorry ... for me."

"I don't, Ken. You're one of the strongest people I've met."

Ken's smile increased. Ian looked at Parrish, admiring the counsellor for the way he'd handled the situation. How did he always know the right thing to do? Ian looked down at his journal, and started writing again. *If I could be like Parrish, I wouldn't have a care in the world. Then I wouldn't be afraid of the pool and the horses and the ghost camp. If only I ...*

As the screen door banged, Ian looked up to see the nurses enter the cabin. "Good morning, everyone!" Nurse Elaine said cheerfully. Her blond hair had been tossed by the wind, and her eyes sparkled. "Can your cabin win the inspection award today?"

"You bet!" Rico exclaimed. "This place is so perfect, it could star in a Mr. Clean commercial."

Both nurses laughed. As everyone watched anxiously, they looked under the beds for dirt, ran their fingers over tables and sills for dust, studied the windows for streaks, and then stopped beside the broom leaning in the corner.

"Naughty, naughty! This should have been put away."

"Come on," Parrish protested. "Give us a break, ladies."

Nurse Elaine smiled. "You guys have done a nice job but one of the girls' cabins is perfect." She gave Parrish a glance, grinning slyly. "The cabin where Dani Darin is a counsellor."

"Oh," he said. "Well, it's nice to lose to real winners." As the nurses left he looked at the broom, feeling guilty, then managed a smile. "Sorry, gang! Maybe tomorrow, right?" Grabbing the handles of Rico's chair he headed quickly outside in the direction of the archery range. His body was tired, and he wanted only to sleep after his late night, but he knew the boys were anxious to get started on their activities.

Winn was already at the archery range. Parrish watched with interest as he used his toes to thread an arrow into a bowstring and carefully drew it back. There was a *twang*, followed by a *thunk* as the arrow dug into the target, quivering.

"Fantastic!" Parrish exclaimed. "That was great, Winn."

He stood up, smiling. "Thanks, but I was aiming for the bull's-eye."

"Oh, well, you'll do better next time."

"Let's see your style."

Parrish threaded an arrow. He sighted along it at the target, which was close enough to score an easy bull's-eye. But then how would Winn feel about being shown up?

"What's the problem?" Winn asked as Parrish lowered the bow, his face thoughtful.

"Nothing. I was, uh, just wondering if there's a wristguard available."

Winn laughed. "What a hotshot!"

Parrish raised the bow again, hoping no one would notice him aiming to the side, and drew back the arrow. Then he remembered Ken, saying not to feel sorry for him. Would Winn know that he'd deliberately missed? Shifting his aim, Parrish let fly. The arrow drove into the heart of the bull's-eye.

"Nice one," Winn said, grinning. "I see I need practice."

Well, Parrish thought, at least this time I didn't make a mistake! Feeling good, he gathered the boys around and gave each one careful instruction, then smiled at the pleasure on their faces as they tried the sport.

Next stop was the Craft House, where Ian began work on a sign for Terry Fox Cabin and the others decided which gifts to make their families. Parrish helped for a while, but his head had begun to throb with pain from his weariness, and eventually he slipped out the back door to look at the lake. The sky was turning dark, and nearby trees and bushes danced in the strong wind that came off the prairie.

Parrish glanced at his watch, happy to know he would soon have his time off. When the craft session ended he helped push wheelchairs to the cabin, trying to ignore his headache, then headed happily for his bed. While Winn and Linda organized a chess tournament he was going to catch up on his sleep.

"Say ... Parrish."

Turning, he saw Ken. The boy was holding some postcards in his shaking hand. "Would ... you write ... these ... for me? I want ... my family ... to ... know ... I'm ... okay."

Parrish fought back a groan, then smiled at Ken. "Sure thing, good buddy. Give me the message for each one, but don't blame me if your family complains about the handwriting!"

It took nearly an hour for Ken to give the messages for his few cards. By the end Parrish couldn't believe the pain inside his head. Then Linda came to him, smiling. "You're looking weary. Why don't you get away from the cabin for a while?"

Parrish hugged her. "Thanks, Linda. I'll see you at lunch."

Outside the cabin Parrish felt elated. Time to himself! He looked up the hillside. Just visible among the thick trees were some old cabins, rarely used since the modern log buildings had been built. Following a trail up the hill, he was soon enclosed in the cool shade of poplars and birches, with the wind shivering the leaves. The sweat on his sticky face slowly dried as he picked some fat blueberries.

"Hello, Parrish."

Whirling around, he saw Clay Croxley approaching. Although Clay was smiling, Parrish dropped the berries. He wasn't doing anything wrong, but he felt uncomfortable under the Director's penetrating gaze.

"How was your first day at camp?"

"Fine thanks, sir."

Clay laughed. "No need to be so formal. We're all friends here."

"Oh, okay. Thanks, uh ... Clay."

"Sorry I snapped at you yesterday, when you had that near-accident with Rico. Tell me, how do you like your boys?"

"Oh, they're all great. Except maybe for Ian."

"Got a problem?"

"He seems very immature. I've tried to help with his fears, but I'm not getting through." Parrish studied Clay's eyes. "Maybe Ian would be happier in a different cabin."

"You want him transferred?"

"Don't get me wrong. It's not for my sake, but I'm sure he'd get along better with another counsellor."

Clay reached for some berries. As he chewed them, his face was thoughtful. Finally he looked straight at Parrish.

"I understand you're hoping to be a teacher?"

Parrish nodded.

"Okay, then here's a lesson for you. Kids can be very difficult to work with. All kids, not just the disabled. It's a tough time for them, coping with all the pressures of growing up. It affects each one in a different way."

"I know that, but ..."

"As older people, we've got to understand what's happening in their heads. When they act strangely, it's up to *us* to display the maturity. That gives them an example of how to act under stress."

Parrish kicked the dirt with his moccasin, avoiding Clay's eyes.

"The one thing we don't do, Parrish, is run

away from a problem. Or ask for an immature boy to be transferred. Right?"

"Yes, sir," Parrish said miserably.

"I don't want to put pressure on you, Parrish, but I *am* watching your performance closely. This is a demanding job, and every counsellor must be tops."

"I know that, sir."

Clay gave his shoulder a squeeze. "I guess this is your T.O., so I won't bother you any longer. Enjoy yourself."

Parrish continued on his way, his head alive with pain. Why had he asked for Ian to be transferred? The idea had just popped into his mind, and it had made him look bad in the Director's eyes. Now the chances of keeping his job as counsellor were worse.

Feeling depressed, Parrish walked on until he came to an old cabin with huge flowers painted on the walls. It was called *The Garden of Sunshine*. Needing a little sunshine in his life, he opened the screen door and immediately laughed. The black eyes of a tiny mouse were staring at him from one of the bunks.

The little creature raced away. Parrish looked at the old furniture and faded green carpet, then lay down on a striped mattress. Despite his worries, he was overwhelmed with a sense of peace as he listened to the wind in the poplars and the sweet sound of birds calling to each other.

Parrish sighed, remembering the tingling sensation he'd felt last night while singing "Taps." *Day is done, gone the sun ...* The words echoed again inside his head, making him smile.

Then, he slept.

FOUR

Ian couldn't eat his lunch.

Right after the meal they'd be leaving for the ghost camp, and his stomach was tight with tension. What would it look like? Would they actually hear the invisible kids singing hymns?

Finally he went alone to the patio, and sat looking at the dark clouds and trees bending low under the strong wind. For a while he hoped the poor weather would force their trip to be cancelled, then he saw the camp bus roll into place behind the Chalet.

There was no sign of Parrish. He'd missed lunch, and was still nowhere in sight to help Linda as she loaded cookout supplies and then helped the kids in wheelchairs into the bus.

Susanna and the others in her cabin arrived, along with their counsellors Speedball and Dani, but still no Parrish. Finally, with everyone on board and the driver impatiently consulting her watch, Clay Croxley came out of the Chalet.

"Problems?" he asked Linda.

Looking embarrassed, she explained that her fellow counsellor was missing. At Clay's suggestion, she and Winn set off to search the upper hillside. Soon they returned with a sleepy-looking Parrish. He mumbled an apology to the Director, who stood with hands on hips, then climbed into the bus to sit beside Dani, the red-headed counsellor. They talked together for a while, then Parrish moved across the aisle to sit with Tracy.

"Nervous about the ghost camp?"

"Are you kidding?" Tracy whispered, then suddenly frowned. "Actually, on second thought, I am kind of scared. I'd feel much better if you'd hold my hand."

As Parrish reached for her tiny fingers, there

were giggles and loud sighs from the other girls.
Feeling jealous, Ian turned to the window as the
bus passed through a small beach community
before climbing a steep hill out of the valley.

"Hey, Winn," Rico called, "why are we taking
the highway to the ghost camp? You said it's on
the same lake as our camp."

"That's right, but there's no road along the
lakeshore. This is the only route for the bus."

"Why didn't we go by boat?"

"They're all being used by kids from other
cabins."

Reaching the open prairie the bus rolled
swiftly along, its passage making wildflowers
dance at the side of the highway. Green fields
stretched to the horizon, the young wheat form-
ing beautiful patterns as it bowed down under
sweeping gusts of wind. Soon they'd passed
through the town of Watrous, its houses and
stores dominated by tall grain elevators, and
were back on the prairie.

"Hi, there."

Ian turned to see that a girl his age had taken
the seat next to him. She had the same straw-
coloured hair as Parrish, but her eyes were a
richer blue. Freckles were scattered across her
nose and cheeks.

"My name's Eleanor, but the kids call me
Blondie."

Ian introduced himself, remembering he'd
seen her loading cookout supplies. "You're
young to be a counsellor."

Blondie laughed. "I just hang around, helping
out. My mom drives this camp bus. I really like
talking to the kids here, because everyone's got a
story to tell." Pointing at a girl in the front, she
lowered her voice. "Except for her."

"Why not?" Ian asked, studying the girl's gentle face with its huge brown eyes. "She looks nice."

"Her family locked her in a closet for five years, until the police found out. She hasn't spoken a word since."

"I don't believe you."

Susanna turned in her seat. "Blondie's telling the truth, Ian."

"But why did they lock her up?"

"She was born with a club foot. Her family thought it was a mark of evil."

"Come on!" Ian protested. "Nobody believes junk like that any more!"

Blondie smiled sadly. "Don't you believe it."

Ian turned and stared out the window.

"Hey, don't be depressed," Susanna said. "Lucy's doing fine. She wouldn't want you feeling sorry for her."

"I can't help it. So many people have problems that it gets me down at times. I wish I could be a really cheerful person like you, but I can't manage it."

"I get depressed, too."

"I doubt it."

Blondie looked at him. "Just this morning, Susanna had a good cry."

"But you're always in such a good mood."

"Sure, but I really need to have a lot of friends, especially since my accident. At first I was just so angry, lying in that hospital bed knowing my back was broken. I screamed at the nurses, but I was so smashed up that no words came from my mouth. It was so terrifying, knowing I'd never walk again. If I could have got some pills, I'd have swallowed them all."

"Now that I don't believe."

"Listen, I really thought my life was over. I'd climbed trees, I'd run and skipped rope. I'd been

free, then suddenly I was trapped. My body
didn't work, and I had to wait for other people to
give me a bath, to dress me, to take me for walks.
Then all I saw everywhere were kids running in
the sunshine."

"I sure know how that feels."

"But suddenly I realized something. *I was
alive.* I'd been spending so much time thinking
about the accident, hating that drunk driver, but
at least I could still *see* those running kids.
That's when I started to get better."

"Then why were you crying this morning?"

Susanna smiled. "I still wish I could walk
again. Maybe bionics will lead to a miracle, I
don't know. Anyway, I try not to let my depres-
sions show because people get turned off. Smile,
and the world smiles with you."

Blondie nodded. "Cry, and you cry alone."

"Unless you've got a good friend like Blondie,
who'll stick by you even when you're down."
Susanna smiled at her with affection. "You
know why I first liked you?"

"Nope."

"Because you asked me why I wear a helmet.
Then you asked how my wheelchair works. You
talked to me like I was just anyone, instead of
pretending I didn't have a handicap in case I'd
get upset."

"That's nice. Want to do something for me?"

"Sure."

"Introduce me to that gorgeous counsellor."

Susanna laughed. "Hey, Parrish, you've got a
fan!"

Turning with a smile, he talked to Blondie for
a while, then joined in a song about baby prunes
as the bus rattled along the dirt road that led to
the ghost camp. Finally, after topping a hill, the
buildings lay waiting.

At first they looked innocent. But it was soon

clear that they had been abandoned. Long tangles of wild grass surrounded them, and loose window shutters banged in the wind as the bus stopped beside a small house with smashed windows. In the yard a rotting sofa was lying on its back.

"This is it!" Winn announced. "Everyone out."

With great reluctance, the campers left the bus. Shivering in the cold wind, they stared at the deserted buildings.

"Where are the ghosts?" Rico asked.

"I don't know." Parrish felt spooked by the wind rushing through the wild grass, and the pounding of wooden shutters against the walls of the old buildings. To his surprise the place gave him the creeps.

"May we ... look ... around?" Ken asked.

"Sure." Parrish pointed at an enormous sagging building that looked like an oversized barn. "Why don't you start there?"

Ken went slowly through the wet grass while the others huddled together, watching. Even Greyeyes, who Parrish had expected to be the bravest, hung back as Ken entered a door under a sign that read *Tabernacle*.

Rico's face was white. "Maybe the ghosts have got him," he whispered after a few minutes, his teeth chattering.

Ian's face was also white. "What's the matter with you?" he said to Parrish. "Aren't you going to go with Ken?"

"Want to come with me?" Parrish asked, but Ian shook his head, looking very frightened.

Winn came to Parrish's side. "We'd better go after him," he said quietly.

"Okay."

As Parrish walked through the long grass he was surprised at how loudly his heart was hammering in his chest. He didn't believe in ghosts, yet there was something eerie about the building.

Something rushed at him out of the darkness. Parrish gasped, then heard the beat of wings as a barn swallow darted out the door. Trying to smile, Parrish looked up at bits of daylight which leaked in through splits in the walls. Then he ran his eyes over a battered old piano.

"Ken?" Winn called softly. "Hey, where are you?"

There was no answer. Parrish was getting worried. He and Winn walked toward a long platform, trying to ignore the moaning of the wind through the cracks in the walls. Loose sheets of paper were being blown around the floor. Parrish saw one was a hymn sheet called *Crown Him King of Kings.*

"Boo!"

Parrish shouted in fear, then turned to see Ken's grinning face. He took a deep breath. "Don't ever do that again. You took twenty years off my life."

Ken laughed. "I was ... hiding. I ... snuck up ... behind you guys. Did you ... ever ... jump!"

Winn laughed, but not very heartily. "It's spooky in here, you know. We'd better get back to the others. They all think you're dead."

Reaching the door of the tabernacle, Parrish looked at the campers clustered together. Their faces changed from anxiety to relief when Ken appeared. Feeling good about their affection for Ken, he watched them crowd forward to ask what happened.

"Hey, Parrish," Winn said quietly, "I've got an idea." He spoke very quickly, then Parrish left the tabernacle and went to join the campers. "Where shall we look next? How about that other big building?"

"I'm game," Greyeyes said. Susanna and

some others nodded agreement, but Ian looked down at his hands.

"You coming?" Parrish asked.

Ian shook his head. His skin had turned bone-white, and fear stared from his eyes. Parrish could see a vein throbbing in Ian's throat. This was the moment of truth for the boy.

"Come on, Ian. If you go into that building, you'll feel a whole lot better about yourself."

Again the boy shook his head. He looked terrible.

"Wait here, then." Parrish turned to the others. They also seemed frightened, but at least they had the courage to enter the creaking old structure. "Let's go."

The building was two stories high. It had once been white, but most of the paint had long ago peeled away from the rotting wooden walls. The remains of two brick chimneys stood up from the roof. Loose window shutters made a frightening *thump-thump-thump* as Parrish led the campers to the door.

The air inside was cold. Creaking and thumping sounds echoed between the walls. Enough daylight came in to show a long room with tables and a kitchen area, where green-grey mold clung to old sinks and a rusting stove.

"Look at the cereal bowls and spoons," one of the girls whispered, pointing at a table. "The kids were eating when the ghosts got them."

"Let's get out of here," Greyeyes said, a tremor in his voice.

"Don't be scared," Parrish said.

Ken picked up a rusty can from the floor, which was littered with junk. "Pea ... soup. Should ... we ... eat it ... for ... supper?"

"Is that a body?" Greyeyes whispered, pointing at a lumpy shape as they entered another large room.

Parrish shook his head. "It's an old mattress."

Something squeaked behind them, making several people jump. But it was only Ian, wheeling into the room. "I changed my mind," he said quietly. "Okay to join you?"

"Sure," Parrish said cheerfully, delighted that Ian had found the courage to enter the building alone. The boy's face was white and his lips were trembling.

"Listen!" Speedball said, raising her hand. "Someone's upstairs."

Everyone was silent, straining to hear above the thumping and creaking of the old building. Parrish heard metal scraping somewhere, but nothing that sounded human.

"Are you sure it was a person, Speedball?"

"Don't forget I'm almost totally blind. My hearing's highly developed. I know I just heard footsteps, somewhere above us."

As every eye went to the ceiling, Corny moaned. Rico's teeth were chattering so loudly that everyone could hear. Ian's breath came in deep gasps. A gust of wind slammed through the old building, shaking it so hard that every shutter rattled, and then they heard the terrible sound.

Somewhere upstairs, a voice was sobbing.

FIVE

Ian screamed.

At the same moment, everyone broke for the door. Susanna reached it first, but Ian grabbed her wheelchair in a panic, pulled her back, and drove his own chair through the opening. Gasping with fear he raced down the hallway.

For a moment Susanna stared after him, too shaken to move, then she also powered her wheelchair out of the room. Meanwhile the sobbing had grown louder. The others cried out as they scrambled for safety.

Only Parrish stayed behind, amazed. He hadn't expected this kind of panic. Maybe Winn shouldn't have sneaked upstairs to do the sobbing, but it was too late now.

The grinning C.I.T. entered the room. "How'd it work?"

"Too well, I think. The kids were petrified. I guess you were too convincing."

"What about Ian?"

"He was the worst, which is a shame. I was so pleased when he found the courage to come in here, but now he's probably feeling terrible."

Outside the building, Linda was rubbing Ian's shoulders as he leaned over a ditch, vomiting. Feeling badly, Parrish called for attention. "Listen, gang, it was all a joke. You only heard Winn sobbing. He snuck up the back stairs."

Dani shook her head. "That was a feeble joke. Look at poor Ian."

As every face swung Ian's way, he shut his eyes and tried to forget the humiliation he'd just suffered. Every kid had heard him scream. Every kid had seen him shove Susanna out of the way. Every kid had watched him throw up.

All because of Parrish.

Rage burned in Ian, remembering the counsellor's fancy talk about facing fear and beating down your demons. Obviously he had set up the whole thing to force him to enter the building. It had worked, all right, but it had worked too well. Now he was a fool in everyone's eyes.

All because of Parrish.

He should never have trusted the counsellor. He should never have liked him. Wiping tears from his eyes, Ian turned his back on the others and rolled away down a bumpy road. Nobody called his name and nobody followed. He sat alone, staring into space.

"Snack time, kids!" Parrish yelled. He waved at Ian. "Come and get it, oldtimer."

Ian sent a dirty look his way. He watched with narrowed eyes as Parrish built a campfire in the middle of the dirt road, then melted a lump of butter in a blackened frying pan. Rico watched Parrish tip out a bowl of batter.

"That stuff looks like white mud. Are you sure you can cook?"

Parrish smiled. "Just watch my smoke, kiddo."

A delicious smell was soon carried on the wind to Ian, but he refused to move as the others crowded around for their pancakes. Maybe they were quick to forgive, but Ian wasn't. Although loud rumbles were coming from his stomach, his face was like stone when Parrish approached with a pancake smothered in butter and maple syrup.

"This is a peace offering, Ian. I apologize."

Ian held out his hand for the plate. Parrish smiled, but the smile disappeared when Ian turned the plate upside down and the pancake dropped into the dirt. "I don't accept your apology."

As Parrish walked quickly away, Ian looked at the others, wondering if they'd been impressed.

But nobody was looking his way. He began to wonder if he'd made a mistake, especially when the cooking utensils were packed away and baseball equipment was taken out. Finally, desperate, he wheeled away in search of berries.

A few grew on a trail that led behind the tabernacle. Ian bumped slowly along, pausing to eat whatever he could find. Soon the other campers were out of sight. To Ian's pleasure, he didn't feel nervous being this close to the ancient black walls of the tabernacle. He continued along the trail until it stopped on a bluff overlooking the lake.

Then he got a shock. Walking along the shore was Parrish.

Ian stared in surprise. A few minutes ago the counsellor had left the group, saying he wanted to explore the old buildings on his own. But that hadn't been true, or he wouldn't be down at the lake. Obviously he was afraid of being seen, because he kept looking over his shoulder while walking quickly along by the water. At last he reached a cabin standing among some trees on the lakeshore, took a final look over his shoulder, and disappeared inside.

So! More information about Parrish's secret. Ian waited patiently for Parrish to leave the cabin, and eventually saw the counsellor reappear. He wheeled quickly back along the trail and was waiting with an innocent face when Parrish made a noisy exit from the tabernacle.

"Sorry to keep you waiting, gang," he said with a hearty laugh. "I just got fascinated."

"What did you find, Parrish?"

"Anything worth telling us about?"

"Nothing much," he said, forcing a smile.

Ian knew the counsellor was hiding something. As they boarded the bus and started for home he tried to guess Parrish's secret. Outside

the window, birds played above the brown fur-
rows of freshly plowed fields; when the bus
slowed at a bend in the road, two large birds
came from the nearby trees to fly about noisily.
Ian realized they were protecting their nest, and
something ached inside him. He couldn't understand the feeling, but it grew stronger when he
looked at a field of wheat caressed by the wind.
He longed to walk among the stalks of wheat
with sun on his face, and birds singing all
around.

Ian's mind remained far away until the bus
entered Watrous and Parrish's loud voice shat-
tered his thoughts. "Hey driver! Please stop at
the Pool Hall."

"Where is it?"

"Up one block, on the right. It's a little red
building with a crooked door."

As the bus stopped, Parrish stood up. "Listen,
gang, I feel like treating you to a game of pool.
Who's in the mood?"

Several people shouted their agreement, but
Speedball said her girls were needed at camp to
set tables for the evening meal. Despite their
disappointment they stayed in the bus, along
with Winn, while the boys from Terry Fox Cabin
got out with eager faces.

Except for Ian. Suddenly a cold wind was
blowing dust into his face, and Parrish was
opening the door of a dark and dingy pool hall.

Linda looked at Parrish. "I'm going to do some
shopping."

"Okay. We'll meet you later at the New
Cameo."

As Linda walked away, Ian felt abandoned.
His skin tingling, he wheeled slowly into the
pool hall. Immediately, his worst fears were
realized.

Teenagers.

A pack of them, with shadowed faces, were gathered at a table where light splashed down on the brightly coloured pool balls. As one teenager bent over the table to fire a savage shot, the others turned to stare. Their faces were hardly visible, but Ian knew what was in their eyes. It would be the same cruelty he'd seen when he entered a video arcade at a mall in Saskatoon and black-jacketed teenagers had turned to stare, then called him names he would never forget.

Cold fear trickled slowly through his body. He watched Parrish walk easily past them, followed by the others. Ken was the slowest. He became the focus of the teenagers' attention, which gave Ian his chance. Swiftly he rolled past Ken and the teenagers. Once safe, he told himself he'd done the right thing in leaving Ken behind. Trying to concentrate on the game, he watched Greyeyes pick up a cue. Supporting it between his chest and the thin arm bent up against his body, he got away a perfect shot, dropping the 3-ball in a corner pocket. Grinning, Greyeyes moved around the table to line up a second shot. At the same moment, Ian glanced at Ken. He was wiping his eyes.

"Beautiful shot!" Greyeyes said. "Didn't I tell you I'm the best?"

Parrish laughed. "Leave some balls for the rest of us."

No one else seemed to be aware of Ken. Ian waited for Greyeyes to take another shot, then wheeled over to him. He turned his face away, but not before Ian saw tears.

"What is it?" he asked.

Ken shook his head.

"Please tell me."

Ken took a deep breath. "One of ... those ... guys ... asked ... if I ... was drunk."

"Drunk?"

"Because ... of how ... I walk." The muscles of his face twisted as he tried to smile. "I don't ... like ... this place."

Ian looked at the teenagers, casually shooting pool as if nothing had happened. "I'm going to tell Parrish," he said, turning toward the counsellor.

"No!"

Startled, Ian turned back to Ken. "Why not? Parrish should stick up for you."

"It's ... my ... problem. I can ... handle ... it."

"What if something else happens? Parrish should be protecting us."

For a moment Ken was silent, as if gathering energy. Then words burst fiercely from him.

"I don't want ... to be ... protected!"

"You're crazy, Ken. Anything could happen."

"I don't ... care!"

Ian looked at Ken's green eyes, trying to think of an argument to change his mind. When his turn came to shoot pool he took a poke at the ball, then returned to worrying about Ken and the teenagers. What if they got vicious?

Parrish looked at Ken. "Ready to try?"

"Okay."

Ken came into the lamp's glow. His eyes were dry as he took the cue. The teenagers grinned as they watched Ken's attempts to control the wavering motion of his cue. A vein throbbed in Ian's throat as he waited anxiously for cruel words. Ken jabbed and thrust without hitting the ball or even coming close. Finally Parrish helped guide the cue, allowing Ken to give the ball a light tap.

The teenagers returned to their game. Ian sighed in relief. That was one danger past, but they still had to reach the safety of the street.

"I'll go pay the bill," Parrish said, when the game was over. "You guys meet me at the door."

The others boys started moving. Ken kept his head up while passing the teenagers, but Ian's eyes were on the floor as he wheeled along, waiting for a word or blow. *Why had Parrish deliberately abandoned them?*

But nothing happened. Although a teenager muttered something, and someone laughed, they reached the front counter without being hurt. Ian's breath escaped in one long sigh, then he leaned forward to look in the glass case.

"Those chocolate bars look pretty good. I'm hungry!"

Parrish took his change from the man behind the counter. "You should have eaten that pancake."

The man leaned on the counter. "What's your name?"

"Ian."

"I guess it's rough being in that wheelchair, Ian. How about if I give you a chocolate bar?"

Ian watched the man's hand move above the chocolate bars. The largest one came out of the case. "Thanks!" he said, accepting it. "That's really nice of you."

Beaming, the man turned to Ken. "I bet you'd like one, too."

"No ... thanks."

"Oh, come on! I've got lots of these things."

Ken didn't reply. Instead, his shaking hand went to the pocket of his jeans. Focusing intently, he managed to get out his wallet. "How much ... is ... the ... bar?"

"Hey there! Put away your money, my friend. For you, it's free."

Ken looked at him. His neck muscles bulged as he spoke. "Thanks ... but ... no thanks." With flailing arms, he headed for the door.

The man winked at Ian. "Can't win 'em all. Now you enjoy that chocolate, little guy."

Ian didn't reply. He managed a faint smile, then wheeled outside into the wind. Parrish and the others were already crossing the street toward the New Cameo restaurant, but Ken was waiting.

"Why'd you turn down the chocolate, Ken?"

There was a long pause. "Other people . . . pay . . . for chocolate . . . bars. Do they . . . get . . . a . . . free bar . . . out of . . . pity?" Tears rose in his green eyes, then rolled down the freckles on his face. Ian made an awkward gesture of support, but Ken waved an angry arm. "Don't . . . you . . . do it . . . too!" Turning, he stumbled away down the street.

Ian watched him go, envying the strength he had just witnessed. Things were a lot worse for Ken than him — with that body he couldn't control — but somewhere he found the steel to get through life.

"You're a lucky man," Ian said, even though Ken was too far away to hear. "I wish I'd been born with your kind of courage."

Across the street, through the window of the New Cameo restaurant, he could see the others. He hesitated about joining them, wondering if there would be cruel remarks about his cowardly behaviour at the ghost camp, then decided to risk it.

The cafe was noisy and crowded. "Hi there!" Greyeyes said with a smile, as Ian wheeled to the table. "Where's Ken?"

"He went for a walk. He'll join us soon."

Parrish held out his hand. "Ian, I want to apologize. I feel responsible for what happened."

Ian stared at the hand, wanting to like Parrish again. "Are you just feeling sorry for me?"

"Of course not, Ian. But I think it's good that

you forced yourself to go somewhere scary."

"Sure, and then look what happened! A real hero!"

Linda reached to him. "Don't feel badly. These things happen."

After a moment's thought, Ian looked at Parrish. "Okay, I guess maybe I accept your apology. But you know what? I want to go back there. Maybe we could do some exploring. There may be some cabins down by the lake worth having a look at."

As he said this, Ian watched Parrish's eyes. Something showed there, maybe panic. Then the counsellor smiled. "Cabins? I doubt it. But perhaps we could return if it's important to you." He looked at Linda. "Do you think it would be okay?"

"I'm not sure." She turned to Ian. "Is it that important to you?"

He thought for a moment, then nodded. "Yes."

"Okay, I'll talk to Clay."

Rico reached for her hand. "Please may we camp overnight?"

"I don't think ..."

"Winn's counsellors let kids camp there. It would be really neat, Linda. Please say yes."

She hesitated, then smiled. "Okay, I'll ask Clay for permission."

Greyeyes whooped with joy. "Dynamite! We'll show those ghosts who's boss."

"Yeah!" Ian shouted, but the word caught in his throat. Trying to disguise his fear, he punched Corny's arm. "What about you? Have you got the guts to face those ghosts while coyotes howl under the moon?"

"You turkey." Corny rubbed his thin arm. "That hurt."

"Turkey! Who are you calling a turkey?"

"You. And you're a wimp, too."

Ian turned to the others, his face horrified. "Did you hear that? I've been insulted." He stared at Corny. "I demand satisfaction. Arm-wrestle me."

"Forget it. You might sue, after I snap your arm like a matchstick."

"Listen to this guy!" Ian crowed. "No guts."

Suddenly Parrish leaned forward, his face hot with anger. "That's enough! If you want to wrestle, try me." As Ian hesitated, Parrish smiled grimly. "Come on, tough guy. Let's have you."

"I'm not sure ..."

"You were ready to wrestle Corny, with his thin arms. Are you scared to take me on?"

"No!" Ian said angrily, reaching out.

Grabbing his hand, Parrish slammed it to the table. His eyes on Ian's face, he watched him struggle to get free, then finally released his grip. Ian threw him a look of hate, then wheeled around to race from the café.

Outside, fury consumed him. Teenagers in a passing car honked and yelled, but he said nothing, all his concentration fixed on the humiliation by Parrish. The camp bus pulled up in clouds of dust and Blondie's mother spoke a friendly greeting, but still Ian sat motionless.

Only Ken was able to reach him. He approached with a smile and squeezed his shoulder with a friendly hand. "How're ... you ... doing?"

"Fine," Ian said, smiling gratefully at Ken. "Thanks for being a friend when I need one."

With the familiar twisting of his facial muscles, Ken grinned. "Any ... time."

The others made a noisy exit from the New Cameo. Soon the bus was rolling home across the prairie in the direction of Little Manitou Lake. Ian stared at Parrish's blond hair and smooth tan, wondering how he could ever have liked him. Then he spoke.

"Got a girlfriend, sir?"

Parrish turned, looking puzzled. "What?"

"You're such a good-looking guy, you must have a girlfriend. Maybe someone who lives around here?"

"Nope."

"This your first time in this area?"

For a brief moment, Parrish hesitated. Then he smiled. "That's right."

"Never been here before?"

The counsellor shook his head.

"Well, how come you knew the pool hall so well?"

Parrish turned to the window, hiding his eyes. "Just a lucky guess."

Ian smiled to himself. "You're a pretty smart guy. Are you planning to be a scientist?"

"No. I'm hoping to be a teacher."

"A teacher? What for?"

"Well, I don't know. I guess because I like kids."

"Are you sure?"

"That I want to be a teacher?"

"No," Ian said. "Are you sure you like kids?"

"Of course I do. Haven't I got along well with you guys?"

"Not particularly."

Parrish turned to look directly at Ian. There was pain in his eyes. "What do you mean by that?"

"You're so impatient with us, and half the time you're so tired you just zombie around the cabin. It's Linda who does everything."

"What about teaching you guys archery?"

"Sure, but that's your job. You get paid to do it."

"You figure I wouldn't do it if I didn't get paid?"

"That's right." Ian knew everyone on the bus was listening, and that he was hurting Parrish, but he couldn't stop himself. "I can't even figure why you took this job. The pay must be terrific."

"It's only okay, Ian. My parents offered me a lot more money to work in their department store, but I wanted to be at Camp Easter Seal. This place is very important to me, but maybe I should quit, since you guys think I'm so useless."

"Hey!" Rico shouted from the back of the bus. "I think you're great, man. Hang in there!"

"Yeah!" Greyeyes said, while Ken leaned forward to pat the counsellor's shoulder. His face brightening, Parrish called cheerfully to Corny for a joke, but Ian still felt he'd got some revenge for the humiliation with the arm-wrestling and the ghost camp.

He smiled grimly, remembering that Parrish would lose his job with a poor performance.

With a little effort, Ian could guarantee that poor performance.

For the first time in his life, Ian felt power.

SIX

Parrish was deeply troubled.

He brooded through the evening meal, then asked Linda if they could talk together. Leaving the boys with Winn at the cabin, they walked to the lake.

"I've really messed up with Ian. The kid hates me, and I feel terrible about it."

"He liked you at the start of camp. What's changed his feelings?"

"I could tell he's a fearful kid, so I've tried to force him to be brave. I wanted him to hold a chicken in his hands but he was too scared, and I guess he felt badly because Dani was watching. I also wanted him to jump into the pool with me but he grabbed his wheelchair brakes and wouldn't let go. The kid's a real mess."

"You're not being fair to him, Parrish. It's his first time away from home. Obviously his parents are overprotective. In many ways he's like a young child, taking his first steps into independence. You have to give him time."

"But I'm just trying to get him started into independence, Linda. It was fabulous today when he forced himself to join us inside that old building at the ghost camp."

"Then things went wrong."

Parrish sighed. "I thought the kids would have a big laugh when they learned it was Winn sobbing upstairs, but all they could think about was Ian, and what he'd done." He picked up a flat stone to skip across the water. "I hope I can patch things up."

"I'm sure you will."

"I'm really anxious to keep this job, Linda. The kids are great to be with." Parrish let fly with another stone and they watched in amazement as it skipped further and further and further out before finally sinking. "That was a champion!"

"When I first met you, Parrish, you said you wanted this job as a reference, to help your chances of getting into teacher training at university. It didn't seem the best of reasons to work here."

"You're right. I'd still like to use Camp Easter Seal as a reference, but something else has happened since I arrived. These buildings, and the lake, and the people, they all make me feel at peace. I feel good about life here. I just hope I don't get fired now that this place has become so important to me."

The camp bell clanged from among the trees. "Time for the talent show," Linda said. As they started back to the cabin she looked at Parrish. "I was so impressed when Ken went into the tabernacle all by himself."

"That kid has real courage. I wish he could lend some to Ian."

"Give him time."

The talent show was held in the dining hall. The tables had been removed, and campers sat in a semi-circle facing an open area in front of the fireplace. Since every cabin would be represented in the show, people talked excitedly about all the performers they'd be seeing. An orange sun, sinking toward the horizon, filled the dining hall with its warm light. Birds in the trees outside added their excited chatter to the voices of campers and counsellors.

"Wait until you see Daphne's magic act!" Susanna called to Parrish and Ian as they looked for a place. "Our cabin's going to take first prize."

"I'm sure you will," Ian replied. "The representative for our cabin is hopeless."

"Hey!" Parrish said sharply. "Don't be so rude."

"I'm sorry," Ian said, "but it happens to be true. He's a real loser."

"Give him a chance. At least he volunteered — and that took courage."

As Ian muttered something Parrish felt suddenly weary. He looked out the side door to some steps which overlooked the lake. Deciding it would be good to rest there for a few minutes, with the cool breeze on his face, he went outside.

He'd only just sat down on the steps when the babble from the dining hall died. Turning, he saw Clay Croxley holding up his hand for attention. "Welcome to an evening of wonderful talent," the black-bearded camp director said with a smile. "Our first act is Ruth Ambler, representing Cabin 10!"

Ruth was brought forward in a wheelchair; like several other campers she had hydrocephalus, which meant her head was very large because of a build-up of fluid. Smiling shyly, she waited until the room was quiet. Then she began to sing. Her voice was so quiet that Parrish had to lean toward her, straining to hear, but the words touched his heart. *"You are my sunshine,"* the girl sang, *"my only sunshine ..."* When it ended there was total silence, then a roar of applause. The girl raised a small hand in thanks.

The next act was a rock group, and the drummer was Winn. Taking the sticks with his toes, he waited while the others strapped on guitars, then opened with a drum roll. The other instruments joined in, blasting the dining hall with their amplified sounds.

Parrish looked across the lake, wondering if the group could be heard on the far shore. The setting sun was haloed in yellow as it dropped toward the hills. Near at hand, the tall pines were silhouetted in black, and a million birds went busily about their lives.

"Hi, Parrish. May I join you?"

Looking up, Parrish saw Dani's smiling face. Sitting down, she stretched out her long legs, then nervously twisted a strand of her soft red hair in one hand.

"You like camp so far?" she asked after an awkward silence.

"No," Parrish said, shaking his head. "I love it."

She laughed. "I wonder ..."

Parrish waited for her question, but Dani seemed to change her mind. Instead she smiled, and pointed at some fat birds. "They look like they're wearing suits, heading home after a hard day at the office."

From behind came loud applause followed by cries of *MORE! MORE!* Parrish turned to smile at Winn, but instead found himself staring into the eyes of Clay Croxley. The man was on the far side of the dining hall, but the frown in those black eyes seared Parrish like a branding iron. He knew the Director was angry because they weren't inside with the kids, but he still turned back to face the lake. Surely counsellors were allowed a bit of time to themselves, and it was so peaceful being with Dani.

"Parrish," she said suddenly, "we're having a family reunion and a big party next weekend. Would you like to come? As my guest?"

"That sounds great, Dani, but why me?"

"Well, because ..." Her blue eyes were fixed on the lake. A blush was slowly spreading across her face. "It's, well, it's because I broke up with my boyfriend. Everyone in my family is feeling sorry for me, and I don't want that during the reunion. So ..." Dani took a deep breath. "So, anyway, you seem really nice, and if you were with me people would feel pleased instead of sorry."

Pleasure fluttered inside Parrish's chest. "Dani, you couldn't have said anything nicer to me."

"So," she said, eyes still on the lake, "you'll come?"

"When is it?"

"Right at the end of this session. We've got a few days off before the next group of campers arrives, so it'll be perfect. My sister and her husband are driving out from the city so they could collect us here. It'll be fun, Parrish."

"I know, but there's a couple of problems."

She turned her eyes to him. "What are they?"

"One I can't discuss, but the second problem is that I might get fired. I'd have to pack up everything to head home." He shrugged. "Maybe you'd better get another guy, Dani. I won't know Clay's decision until the last day of camp."

"I think I'll risk it. Clay isn't going to get rid of you."

"I'm not so sure," Parrish said, remembering the searing look he'd just received. "Maybe I'd better go mingle with the kids, before Clay writes me off."

Ian watched Parrish come inside, smiling happily, and jealousy cut through him like a knife. The counsellor had everything — good looks, perfect health, a gorgeous red-headed girlfriend, and not a worry in the world. It didn't seem fair that some people got the best of life, while others had a bad deal from birth. He tore his eyes away from the counsellor and tried to concentrate on a boy playing the bongos with artificial hands. The music was good, and the crowd was loving it, but Ian burned with jealousy. He wished desperately that the feeling

could end, but he didn't know how to make it end.
Twisting the wheels of his chair, he headed
outside. The air was cool. A sweet breeze played
around his face as he rolled across the patio. He
didn't know where he was going, he just needed
to be alone.

But he wasn't. Around a corner of the Chalet
he found Corny with tears in his eyes. For a
moment Ian hesitated, then powered past. *Let
him suffer*, he thought, *he deserves it*. He raced
to the end of the ramp, then stopped to look back.

Corny's thin body was slumped down in his
chair. Everything about him sagged. Even the
wheelchair seemed dejected. *He's alone*, Ian
thought, *just like me*. Like a cloud suddenly lifting, his own turmoil disappeared. Quickly
wheeling forward, he stopped by Corny.

"What is it, Corny?"

The boy shook his head. "Go away," he
muttered.

"Is it okay if I sit here for a few minutes?"

Corny's eyes blazed. "No! Get out of here, you
stupid wimp."

Ian reached out a hand to touch Corny but the
boy shook it off.

"Beat it, you creep! I want to be alone."

When Ian didn't move, Corny started to wheel
away. But Ian reached out quickly to hold his
chair. "Before you go, I want to say I'm sorry."

"Leave me alone."

"Listen, Corny, I've been a rat."

Corny turned to Ian. His eyes were filled with
tears. "You sure are a rat. You've ruined my time
at camp, and I've been looking forward to it for
months."

Ian sighed deeply. "I'm sorry, Corny. I know
I've been a real jerk, but I've been scared, and ...
I guess I didn't want anyone to know."

"You scared? That's a laugh."

"I mean it."

"With all those muscles, and your blond girl-friend on the bus? What have you got to be afraid about? I've got nobody."

"Let me be your friend." As Corny hesitated, Ian held out his hand. "Please help me." Again there was hesitation, then Corny smiled faintly.

"Okay," he said quietly.

"Thanks, Corny. That means a lot."

"I'm probably making a big mistake."

Ian smiled. "Want to go back inside?"

"No."

"How come?"

"Because I wish I hadn't volunteered for the talent show. I'm going to make our cabin look bad."

"Nonsense. You don't want to miss performing for such a big audience."

"My jokes stink."

"No, they don't. People laugh at them. Rico even writes them down. I memorized some to tell my folks when I get home."

"Liar." Corny leaned back in his chair to gaze at some birds playing in a stand of poplars. "Which jokes did you memorize?"

"The one about the tailor making trousers last, and that great riddle about an umbrella going up when the rain comes down. Plus the knock-knock joke."

Corny smiled. "No need to cry about it."

"That's the one! Come on, let's go inside. We're missing all the acts." Wheeling across the patio, Ian was pleased to hear the squeak of Corny's wheelchair close behind. His heart felt light as he entered the dining hall. Going to Linda, he whispered something in her ear. Then, when Cabin 8's turn was announced, it was Ian who wheeled forward.

"Ladies and gentlemen," he said, surprised at

the strength of his voice, "It's with great pleasure that the boys of Terry Fox Cabin present,
for your pleasure and gratification, the many
talents of a comic genius. Please welcome
warmly ... Canada's very own ... *Corny
Newman!*"

As loud applause rang out, Corny came forward looking thrilled. He gave Ian a quick smile,
then turned to his audience. "What happened to
the kid who ran away with the circus? They
made him give it back!"

Laughter, and Corny beamed.

"What date is a command? March fourth!"

"Go for it, Corny!" Rico called from the
audience.

"What did the big chimney say to the little
chimney? You're too young to smoke."

Feeling great, Ian enjoyed the rest of the show
immensely. Clay Croxley also looked pleased as
he came forward at the evening's close to con-
gratulate the performers. Then he made an
announcement.

"Each summer a special race is held at the
beach community down the road from camp. It's
called the I-Think-I-Can Relay. Last year it was
a very close race. It looked like Watrous High
School would win, but in the last leg the lead
changed hands, and the victory went to Camp
Easter Seal!" Cheers, whistles and foot-
stomping interrupted Clay. "This year's relay
takes place in three days. Tomorrow there will be
camp try-outs for runners, swimmers, cyclists
and paddlers. Campers and counsellors are eligi-
ble, so let's have a big turn-out."

Clay paused, looking around at the campers'
faces.

"Are we champions?"

"YES!!" roared all the voices.

SEVEN

Close to dawn, the air was filled with bird song.

Ian was awake because something was wrong — Greyeyes was making no effort to train. Last night he'd announced plans for a dawn run to get in shape for the relay try-outs, but he was still asleep. Parrish had promised to wake him, but he'd crept into the cabin late last night and was still snoring noisily.

So it was up to Ian. He hesitated, feeling sleepy, then thought of Greyeyes winning the relay for Camp Easter Seal. Pulling on his clothes, he wheeled quietly across the cabin.

"Hey, Greyeyes, wake up! You've got to train."

He sat up. "I almost forgot!" Pulling on his clothes, he headed for the door. Ian started back to bed, then decided to watch Greyeyes' training methods. The air outside was clean and cold, making him shiver. To the east the sky was a pale blue with a covering of ragged pink clouds, and the metallic surface of the lake was rippled by wind. The birds were everywhere, playing in the sky or singing from trees.

Greyeyes did deep knee-bends, then lay down on the cold concrete for a few sit-ups. "Thanks for your help," he said, starting away. "See you later."

"Good luck!"

It was delightful to be outside with the world entirely to himself, so Ian decided to wait for Greyeyes' return. He rolled back and forth along the ramp, seeing what speed he could manage, then sat back to sniff the cold air.

At last the thump of feet sounded along the ramp, then Greyeyes appeared with his familiar brown headband. "Hi," he said, gasping for air. "That was ... some run."

"Where'd you go?"

"Down ..." Greyeyes sucked in the cold air, catching his breath. "Down past those beach houses. I didn't see anyone, except some old dog."

"Was his name Parrish? I hate that guy."

"He's not so bad. You've just got a grudge."

Greyeyes watched with interest as Ian kept his wheelchair tilted back while turning in a circle, then changed direction to make another circle. "That's a good trick."

"Thanks," Ian said proudly. "Practice makes perfect."

"Why are you in that chair?"

"I was born with spina bifida." Ian leaned forward. "Can you feel those two big lumps at the bottom of my spine?"

"Yes."

"I've got no sensations lower than that."

"So I could kick you in the leg, and you wouldn't feel it?"

"That's right," Ian said, laughing, "but you'd feel it when I socked you in the jaw."

"I surrender," Greyeyes said with a laugh. For a minute he looked at the lake, thinking. "That was a good talent show. You should have been our cabin's rep."

"Doing what?"

"Your crab-walk across the floor on your hands."

"Aw, that's nothing. Corny's jokes are better."

"That kid is nuts."

"You think so?"

"He's totally weird. I'd let the air out of his wheels if they weren't solid rubber, just like his head."

Ian laughed uncomfortably. He started to reply, then tilted back his wheelchair and did a slow circle while he tried to think of words to say in Corny's defence.

"So," Greyeyes said, "the ghost camp tomorrow night. Maybe we'll see some wispy kids streaming through the tall grass, singing hymns."

Ian shivered. "It's cold out here. I think I'll go inside."

Greyeyes laughed. "Scared of ghosts?"

"Of course not. I can't wait to go back. Wasn't it my idea?"

"That's true," Greyeyes admitted. "Listen, maybe we could set up a gag to scare the life out of old Corny. Then there'd be another ghost kid!"

"Yeah, I guess ..."

"What's wrong with you? I think it's a great idea."

"Well, let's wait and see."

Greyeyes went inside. Ian was about to follow when he heard someone approaching. Along the ramp came Clay Croxley, a puzzled smile on his face. "Up already?"

"I'm helping Greyeyes train for the relay. He's just been for a run."

"Good. I'll see you later."

Suddenly, Ian gave in to temptation. "Are counsellors allowed to have girlfriends, Clay?"

"What do you mean?"

"Well, I just wondered. If counsellors sneak off at night to visit a girlfriend, well it's pretty rough on the campers, because the counsellors zombie around next day without getting involved in the activities."

Clay frowned. "Are you talking about Parrish?"

Ian swallowed, and looked down. "Uh ..."

"Please answer me."

"Well," Ian muttered, "I don't know if Parrish has a girlfriend. But he was sure out late last night."

"How late?"

"One o'clock. I looked at my watch when he came in." Ian studied the man's face. Nothing showed, but he knew there'd be trouble for Parrish. He tried to feel good about this, remembering how he'd been humiliated by the counsellor, but he couldn't. "Maybe," he murmured, "maybe I got the time wrong."

Clay didn't respond. Instead he walked away deep in thought. Feeling terrible, Ian returned inside to lie down.

But he couldn't sleep.

Finally, after a long wait, the wake-up call was delivered by Nurse Elaine and Nurse Louise. Parrish dragged himself out of bed, looking like a bear with a sore head, and gave orders in a cranky voice. At breakfast a cup of coffee seemed to improve things slightly, but he still looked gloomy during the songs that followed the meal.

"Okay," Linda said when the singing ended, "it's clean-up time. Then we're going riding."

A chill ran through Ian. "Riding?"

"You bet!"

"Oh. Well, uh, that's great."

The stable and riding trails were located in the woods. When they reached them, the boys were told to wait while a dark-haired girl, wearing jeans and a *University of Saskatchewan* T-shirt, led a brown horse from the stable. It was snorting and throwing its head about, but the girl spoke soothingly as she led it in their direction. Ian backed away as the horse went by, kicking up stones with its powerful-looking hooves. The girl stopped it by a platform, then Linda pushed Rico's wheelchair up a ramp to the top of the platform.

"Great, man!" There was a huge grin on Rico's face as Linda lowered him to the saddle and he was handed the reins. "Hey! I've never steered a horse before."

Linda laughed. "Then I'm coming along for the ride."

As they disappeared among the trees, Ian saw Winn coming his way. "How're you doing, Ian?" the C.I.T. asked.

"Okay I guess."

"I stopped at the Craft House this morning to look at your Terry Fox sign. You've got the touch of an artist."

"Thanks!"

"Have you heard the nurses are sponsoring a kite contest? A prize for best design, and another for the kite that stays up the longest."

"I'd like to enter. I love this camp, Winn. When I think how homesick I was when we first met, I can't believe it."

"It's too bad what happened at the ghost camp. I feel badly."

"It's wasn't your fault. I blame Parrish."

"Well, you shouldn't. I set up the gag."

"Sure, but it was Parrish who kept bugging me to go into that building. Then I behaved like an idiot." Anger flared inside Ian, and for a minute he felt better about betraying Parrish's late night to Clay Croxley. Then, as guilt returned, he concentrated on watching the slow process of getting Corny onto a second horse. "Probably we won't all get a chance to ride. We're playing basketball at ten o'clock."

"Don't you want to go riding?"

"Sure, I can't wait! But my stomach is giving me trouble today."

Rico's horse came out of the woods. As Linda looked for another rider, Ian pretended to clean his fingernails. "You're next, Ian!"

He smiled at her. "Thanks, but Ken can have my turn."

"He'll go after you."

"What about Greyeyes?"

"Same thing."

"Oh." Ian glanced at Winn, and saw his watching eyes. "Okay," he said quietly, "but only a short ride." With shaking hands he wheeled to the ramp. Up close, the horse was huge.

The ramp was too steep for Ian to manage alone, so Linda called to Parrish for help. He'd fallen asleep under a tree, and looked cranky as he approached. Ian closed his eyes, praying for courage as his wheelchair was pushed up to the platform.

The dark-haired girl was holding the bridle. "Ever ridden before?"

Ian shook his head.

"Nervous?"

He swallowed. "No," he said, then flinched as the horse tossed its head. "It looks like fun."

"Just let Gypsy know you're the boss."

"Okay." He stared at the muscles under the horse's shining brown coat. "No problem."

Parrish helped Ian onto the saddle. He grabbed it with both hands, then felt slightly better when Parrish got on behind him. The girl handed Ian the reins. "Good luck!" She stepped back, but the horse didn't move.

"Go," he said nervously, trying to sound like the boss. "Hee. Haw."

The girl slapped the horse on the rump. It snorted, then started walking. Ian's body began to bounce around. "You okay?" Parrish asked from behind.

"S-s-sure," he said, his teeth clicking together with the horse's motion. "It's eas-s-s-y."

"Then let's go faster." Parrish's feet thumped against the horse, and suddenly Ian's body was jerking wildly as the horse shot ahead. It was heading straight for a group of trees, but Parrish pulled on the reins and they swerved to the right. "Still okay?"

"No! I'm scared!"

Parrish pulled on the reins. Immediately the horse slowed to a peaceful walk. Ian began to relax as he realized the horse could be controlled so easily. After a minute he reached for the reins. As they approached a bend in the trail, he pulled on the reins and was amazed when the horse turned. "It works! I did it!"

Parrish laughed. "You'll be cow-punching in no time."

Ian leaned forward to stroke the stiff black hairs of the horse's mane, then settled back in the saddle to listen to the creak of leather and the rustle of the poplars which surrounded the trail. "This is fun, Parrish."

"Good man," he said, squeezing Ian's shoulder.

As he'd been doing all morning, Ian tried to avoid the memory of betraying Parrish's late night to Clay Croxley. Then, summoning all his courage, he decided to apologize. "Listen, I ..."

"Just a second, Ian." Parrish reached for the reins to stop the horse. The counsellor looked down the hill past the poplars to a small group of girls approaching the riding area. "There are the kids who went to the ghost camp with us. I'm thinking of inviting them along when we go back. What do you think of them?"

"They seem nice. Why?"

"What about their counsellors?"

Shining in the sun was Dani's long red hair. Ian stared at her, filled with jealousy, and then shrugged his shoulders. "She's okay, if you like the type."

"What's that mean?"

"Nothing," Ian muttered. "Let's finish this stupid ride."

"What's wrong with you? I thought we were having fun."

Ian couldn't find any words to answer.

* * *

At the basketball court, Parrish lay down again. He was drifting off to sleep when a strange feeling disturbed him. He sat up, and discovered he was being watched by Clay Croxley.

The Director stood on the far side of the basketball court. Parrish managed a weak smile, then shifted his eyes and pretended to be involved in the game. "Nice try!" he called to Rico, as the boy got off a shot that hit the metal hoop before bouncing to Ken.

"Me! Me!" Corny screamed. "Pass it to me!"

"I'm in the clear!" Ian cried. "Pass it here!"

Parrish stood up, trying not to look at Clay, and went to the side of the court. He waited until a shot bounced out of bounds, then motioned for the ball. "All right, I've studied you all in action. Now I'm going to give you some tips."

"But Linda already taught us," Ian protested.

"Sure, and she did a fabulous job. But basketball is a man's sport."

"We just want to play."

Rico nodded his head. "Right."

"You don't want to learn basketball from a champion?"

"No," Ian said. "We just want to have fun."

Parrish felt his face burning, but fought back his anger and hurt. Handing the ball to Linda, he returned to the side of the court while the boys screamed for a pass. A moment later, Clay Croxley walked over. "Good morning. How are you feeling?"

"Oh, fine," Parrish said, trying to sound cheerful.

Clay folded his arms across his chest as he watched the basketball game. Parrish felt jealous of Linda who already had the boys playing at a respectable level. "The kids are great at archery, too. They were a little awkward at first but I got them going without too much trouble."

Clay nodded. "What time did you get in last night?"

Parrish stared at the director, caught off guard. "Well, uh, I guess around 10:30." Clay was silent. "Um, maybe it was eleven."

"Are you sure it wasn't one a.m.?"

Parrish dropped his eyes, wondering how Clay had found out. "Maybe," he murmured. "I can't remember."

Clay waited for Parrish to raise his embarrassed eyes. "This is a demanding job, and counsellors don't get much time on their own. But you must get your rest. If that requirement is too difficult, you should consider resigning."

"But I love it here."

"Then no more late nights. Is that clearly understood?"

Parrish nodded his head, feeling numb.

Clay waited for a break in the basketball action, then complimented the boys on their game. He went over to Linda, and they talked quietly together. Parrish watched their conversation, feeling glum, then went on court to encourage the boys as they played.

To his pleasure, making the effort greatly improved his spirits. He was feeling good when everyone assembled later for the relay try-outs. The event of special interest was the foot race between two of his favourite people, Winn and Greyeyes.

All the boys from Terry Fox Cabin were at the boathouse, which marked the finish line for the race. Suddenly other people, who were spread out along the route from the camp gates, began to cry out encouragement. For a moment Parrish saw nothing. Then he glimpsed Greyeyes, pulling away from the pack of runners with Winn at his side.

The faces of the two showed total concentration as they left the other runners behind. For a moment it seemed they would finish in a dead heat, but Greyeyes found an extra burst of energy to hit the tape just ahead of Winn.

"Great race!" Ian shouted. "I've been helping Greyeyes to train, you know," he said to Nurse Elaine who was standing beside him.

"You must be a good trainer," she smiled, "because Winn has won this race for the past couple of years."

Nurse Louise nodded. "Greyeyes is good, but he'll be up against some great runners. The guy from Watrous High School is really good."

"No sweat," Ian said, grinning. "My boy Greyeyes can lick anyone."

That evening, with the words of the last song echoing inside his head, Parrish pushed Ian's wheelchair onto the patio. The sky was filled with a weird orange light caused by the sun setting behind black rain clouds. Fat raindrops fell straight down, soaking Parrish and Ian as they raced along the ramp.

"This is fun!" Ian yelled. "It's chariot time!"

Reaching the cabin, Parrish grabbed a towel and rubbed Ian's head, feeling like a father. Then he grinned at the others as they burst in through the door. "Song time, Linda!"

She grabbed her guitar. "*Were you ever in Quebec ...?*"

"*... stowing lumber on the deck ...* join in, guys!"

"*Heigh ho and away we go, riding on a donkey ...*"

Everyone sang loudly and happily, the boys and counsellors ignoring their wet clothes. Then Rico opened the book-bag on his wheelchair and pulled out a pancake. "Anyone hungry?"

"Where'd you get that?" Parrish asked, laughing.

"At breakfast. It seemed too good to waste."

"Toss it here!" Corny shouted. "I'll eat anything."

Rico whipped the pancake across the cabin like a Frisbee. Corny tried to catch it but missed, and the soggy mess smacked into his face. He roared with laughter, then looked at his glasses. "If they'd been broken, my Dad would've flipped."

"Anyone thirsty?" Parrish asked, pulling a giant Thermos from under his bed. "I brought us all some hot chocolate from the kitchen."

As the boys crowded around, Parrish smiled happily. He wanted the time to last forever, but eventually the campers were tucked away and he lay down under his blanket. His eyes studied the pattern thrown on the ceiling by the yellow porch light as he fought off sleep. Eventually, after what seemed like hours, the screen door creaked open to admit Clay Croxley on his nightly rounds. Parrish closed his eyes, pretending to be asleep, until the Director left.

Fifteen minutes later, he got up and left the cabin. The rain had stopped, but the ground was slippery underfoot as he trotted quickly in the direction of the open prairie. Reaching a path which had become familiar to his feet, he broke into a run.

From somewhere in the night came the lonely whistle of a freight train. Parrish knew he was breaking Clay's rule and his life at Camp Easter Seal could be ending, but still he ran on until at last he saw the cabin waiting beside the lake.

Reaching the door, he knocked lightly. "It's me," he called.

For a moment he felt great fear because there

was no reply. Then he opened the door and received a welcoming smile from the person who was waiting.

"Parrish," she said gently. "I thought you weren't coming."

EIGHT

For the first time, Ian was not aware of Parrish's late-night absence from the cabin. Exhausted and happy after the day's events, he'd slept deeply from the moment his head touched the pillow.

In the morning, after breakfast, he watched with pride as his sign reading TERRY FOX CABIN was hammered to the porch wall by Linda and Parrish.

"That's a good painting you did of Terry," Corny said. "I'd know those curls anywhere."

"Thanks!"

The others also congratulated Ian. Then Parrish grinned. "Who's for skinny dipping?"

"What's that, man?" Rico asked suspiciously.

"Nude swimming. We're due at the pool this morning. It might be fun to go swimming without our suits."

"Forget it!"

Parrish laughed. "Okay, if that's how you feel." He turned to Ian with a smile. "Going to try swimming today, oldtimer?"

Ian shook his head. "I'm — I'm due, uh, at the Pillbox for my treatment with Aerie-Phenom."

"Can't you do that later?"

"Not if we're going to the ghost camp."

"I'd forgotten that." Parrish shook his head. "Well, I'm disappointed. I'd really hoped to get you into the pool today."

"Maybe another time," Ian murmured. He hurried into the cabin for his journal, then set off for the Pillbox, which was the name of the cedar-log building where the nurses were located. When he went inside Nurse Elaine was waiting with a smile.

"You remind me of my mom," Ian said. "She's super pretty, too."

"I bet she'd love to hear that. Have you been writing home?"

"Sure thing, and I got a letter from my folks today. It sounds like they miss me."

The air inside the Pillbox was clean and fresh. They went down a corridor to a room with twin beds and a window overlooking the lake. "You know," Ian said, "It's still hard to believe you're a nurse."

"Why's that?"

"Because you wear T-shirts and cut-offs instead of a uniform. And because it doesn't smell like a hospital in here."

She laughed. "I can put on a white dress if you want, but these clothes make it easier to nurse on the floor if someone comes in with a foot problem."

"Weird!" Ian said, laughing. "This place is crazy."

"I see you brought your journal. You can write about the wild and crazy nurses of Camp Easter Seal during your treatment."

"Good idea," Ian said, but after a few minutes he found he was writing instead about his fear of the ghost camp. *There is nothing worse than being afraid,* he wrote. *It makes me a slave. It makes me want to hide in a place where no one can see my face. It makes me ashamed.*

But the words couldn't take away the fear. When he was finished at the Pillbox he went to the pool, where he sat in wretched silence listening to the delighted screams of campers being attacked by a killer shark named Parrish.

"Shark hungry!" The counsellor's brown body slipped beneath the water, then suddenly reappeared beside Ken. "Shark eat boy, taste good."

"Help!" Ken yelled, laughing as Parrish's teeth dug into his arm. He slapped at the water and managed to get some into the attacker's eyes. "Rico ... Greyeyes ... someone ... help!"

I'd like to help, Ian thought miserably, *but I'm sitting here like a wimp.* Suddenly he decided to try the pool, but at that moment a whistle blew. "Time's up!" called Kathy McMaster, the swim instructor. "Everyone out."

As moans and groans sounded, Parrish launched a final attack and then helped the boys out of the pool. As Ian tried to ignore their joy he saw Linda returning from her time off.

"Come help prepare the supplies, Ian. We're leaving soon for the ghost camp."

"Are we still staying overnight?"

She nodded. "You don't sound very happy about it. I thought it was your idea to go back there."

Ian looked down at his hands. "But not overnight."

Linda knelt beside his wheelchair. "You'll be safe, Ian."

"I know," he said, blushing. "But I'm scared anyway."

She smiled. "Telling me about your fear is a big step forward, Ian. Congratulations."

He looked at her. "Do you mean that?"

"Of course. Now come on, let's get to work."

Linda's praise made all the difference to Ian, who felt good until the moment the bus approached the ghost camp and he saw the old buildings again. Then he shivered, wishing they could return to the safety of Terry Fox Cabin.

"Everybody out!" Speedball shouted, as the bus came to a stop. "First job is to pitch tents."

Soon the big canvas tents were being unrolled over the long grass. Swarms of mosquitoes surged out of hiding to surround the workers, who yelled at each bite and slapped fiercely at their exposed skin. As each tent roof was hoisted into place, pegs were pounded into the ground for support ropes.

Ian did his best to help, but it was hard to keep his eyes off the decaying black wood of the buildings. They creaked and groaned in the wind while birds flew in and out the empty windows. Finally he wheeled to the cooking pit, where Dani and Speedball were preparing a fire.

"What's for supper?"

"My famous Kung-Fu Stew," Dani replied. "You haven't lived until you've tried it."

"You haven't died until you've tried it, either," said Speedball. "Dani and I went to Guide camp together. She practised the fine art of poisoning on me too often."

"Feeling nervous about spending the night here, Ian?"

"Of course not." He glanced up at the sky, where a big bird with outstretched wings hovered far above. "Isn't that beautiful? What kind of bird is it?"

"Looks like a red-tailed hawk, searching for mice and gophers."

"How can it see them from way up there?"

"That's the miracle of life." Dani smiled at him. "How'd you like to be a gopher?"

"And get eaten by a hawk? Forget it."

"You're too nice to be eaten, Ian, so why not go-fer some wood to build up this fire."

"You bet!" Ian said, laughing. He began gathering old shingles and broken boards from the wild grass and soon had a nice pile beside the cooking pit. When the stew was served later he felt he'd made a personal contribution to the pleasure of the others.

Everyone huddled close to the fire while eating. The red and orange flames threw their light as far as the old buildings, which watched silently.

Suddenly, Ian pointed. "Look!"

All heads snapped toward the tabernacle. "What is it?" Speedball cried. "What do you see?"

"That shape," Ian said frantically. "There, inside that door, what is it?"

Linda took a few steps toward the building. "It's just shadows, Ian, but they do look human."

"I think it's someone with an axe."

She laughed and walked quickly through the darkness all the way to the building, then went inside. "It's okay!" she called, her voice carried on the wind. "Nobody's chopped off my head."

"Come back!" Rico yelled. "We're scared for you."

When Linda reached the campfire Ian looked at her with respect. "Wow. Are you brave!"

"Thanks, Ian. Say, who knows a good ghost story?"

When there were no volunteers, Dani looked around the circle of faces. "I could tell you about something that happened to me. A year ago I was babysitting at a neighbour's house. A terrible wind started to blow, and I kept hearing these branches scratching against an upstairs window. It got so noisy that I finally went upstairs to look at the tree. *But there wasn't one.*

"Suddenly the lights went out. I tried the phone, but it was dead. Deciding to go for help, I got the baby, then went outside into the darkness. A huge mansion stood alone in the distance. As I gazed at it, wondering if someone there could help, I heard the terrible sound of heavy breathing."

For a moment Dani was silent. "I'll never

forget that breathing. It was everywhere, surrounding me, pressing closer and closer, and then suddenly, I was running. The baby was crying, and I was running toward that distant house, knowing I had to escape.

"My legs wouldn't move fast enough. It was like running through molasses. Finally I reached the horrible old mansion. There were dead trees in the yard, and a man in black clothes stood by the door. I cried to him for help, but he only stared at me as I ran inside."

Dani's voice was shaking. "A staircase was close by and I ran to it, still feeling this thing behind me. Upstairs the air was dark and clammy as I looked desperately for some place to hide. Then I saw an open door. I ran inside. The baby had stopped crying, but I could still hear something coming slowly along the hallway, searching."

Dani shivered. "As the thing came closer I knew it was all over for me. I opened my mouth to scream as the breathing filled the room. The thing was coming for me. Closer and closer it came, then reached out. 'Tag,' the creature said. 'You're it!'"

For a moment there was total silence around the campfire, then Parrish roared with laughter. Ian stared at Dani's smiling face. "What a fantastic story! I was having a nervous breakdown."

"Want another?"

Rico held up his hand. "No way! I've had enough ghosts to last me a lifetime."

Ian tried to ignore the sound of the long grass being shivered by the wind and the banging of the shutters against the old buildings, hidden now in the darkness beyond the red glow of the embers.

"Let's all join hands," Speedball said. When

the group had linked hands, she led the singing:

> Friends, friends, friends
> We will always be;
> Whether in fair
> Or in dark stormy weather,
> Camp Easter Seal
> Will keep us together.

Ian remembered when these people had been frightening strangers. Now they were friends sharing this peaceful moment, their faces lit by the warm glow of the embers. He was sure he saw tears in Susanna's eyes, and Parrish looked happier than ever before.

Then the moment ended and they started toward the tents. Parrish and Linda clicked on flashlights and the boys fell in close to the beams, feeling cold and nervous as they left the fire. The buildings creaked and thumped nearby.

"Look at that." Parrish pointed at a misty halo encircling the moon. "They say a moon like that sets werewolves free to roam."

Total silence from the boys.

Inside a nearby tent, the girls could be heard talking as they prepared for sleep. Ian left his wheelchair by the entrance to the boys' tent and manoeuvred his way to his sleeping bag. Pulling a blanket to his chin, he inhaled the smell of canvas and listened to the wind.

Linda put her flashlight beside the tent flap. "I'll leave this here. We'll be at the fire for a while."

"Do you have to go?" Corny asked nervously.

"We won't be far," Parrish answered. "If anything happens, just scream."

"Ha, ha," Corny muttered unhappily.

"Good night, all," Linda said. "Sleep tight."

"Don't let the vampires bite," Parrish added.

The flap closed behind the counsellors. Ian tried not to think about the buildings close by, but the shutters could be heard thumping.

"Listen!" Corny said. "Isn't that ghost kids, singing hymns?"

His nerves prickling, Ian sat up. The other boys shifted anxiously in their sleeping bags, then Ken's voice came out of the darkness. "We'd ... have ... to hear ... the piano. Ghost ... kids ... can't ... sing ... without it."

"Are you sure?"

"Of ... course."

"Okay," Corny said. "I know I didn't hear a piano."

For a long time the boys were silent, then the sound of deep breathing was heard as they drifted off to sleep. Ian was still staring into the dark air when a hand touched him. "You awake?" Greyeyes whispered. "Now's the time to get Corny!"

"How?"

"You know that wrecked sofa by the house? I saw some old clothes in the grass beside it."

"So what?"

"Ssh, not so loud! We can use the clothes to make up a dummy, then put it under Corny's blanket. He'll wake up, and think there's a ghost beside him!"

"Good idea," Ian whispered. "Get the clothes, and I'll help make the dummy."

"No way I'm going near those buildings."

"But it's your idea!"

"You do it, Ian. You've got more guts than me."

"Do you think so?"

"Sure. Go get the clothes, and let's freak Corny out of his mind."

Ian was surprised and pleased that Greyeyes thought he had courage. Even though the joke was a bit mean to Corny, and made him feel uncomfortable, it would be a real test to go for those clothes. Finally, feeling extremely nervous, Ian got dressed and pulled himself across the tent. Getting into his wheelchair, he picked up the flashlight.

"Wish me luck," he whispered, but only a sleepy mumble came from Greyeyes.

Ian felt less nervous when he saw the beauty of the wild grass, now a soft silver under the moon. In the distance were the black silhouettes of the counsellors around the fire, and he heard Parrish's laughter carried on the wind.

Forcing a path through the wild grass, Ian found the scattered clothing near the sofa. His nose wrinkled when he reached for a shirt and discovered it was wet and slimy.

"It's not fair to play this trick on Corny," Ian whispered to himself. "I can't betray him — he's my friend." Dropping the slimy shirt, he looked at the tabernacle. The old walls were a strange colour under the moonlight. The building sagged so much it looked ready to collapse, but he still wondered what was inside. If a person could find the courage to enter that place, a person could do anything. Reaching for the wheels of his chair, Ian went quickly toward the building. Then his view of the counsellors' fire was cut off, and he stopped.

He was alone.

His stomach turned cold. He started to turn back, then shook his head angrily and wheeled forward. Reaching the door, he quickly switched on the flashlight. The beam swept across the dirt floor, picking out the shape of pews and some white sheets of paper being blown about by the winds.

Then he saw the piano, and an idea formed in his mind. As his pulse raced Ian sat staring at the piano, feeling terribly afraid and terribly excited. *Do it!* Taking a deep breath, he wheeled toward the piano and pushed down on a key. Only a hollow thump sounded. The moaning of the wind threatened to drive Ian back to safety, but he'd come too far to fail now.

Ian selected another key. This one produced a high-pitched ting. He hit it again and then some others. Then he ran his hand the length of the keyboard, hearing loud notes ring out. He paused, hit several keys, and began to sing.

"Onward Christian soldiers," his voice cried out, at first shaky and then gaining strength, *"marching as to war, with the Cross of Jesus going on before."*

That was all he could manage. His own words filled him with fear. They echoed inside the walls, seeming to stir up the souls of the dead. Taking his hands away from the keyboard, he was about to quit when he heard Rico's voice.

"Help!" he was shouting. "Help, ghosts!"

"Save us!" another voice cried, distorted by terror. "Please, help us!"

"Linda!" a voice screamed, and this time he recognized Corny. "Save me! Save me!"

Loud cries were coming from the girls' tent, adding to the bedlam. His own fear completely forgotten, Ian pounded the keys and kept singing. Outside, flashlight beams cut the night as counsellors ran to the tents. Another beam flicked along the wall to the piano. Loud laughter followed.

"It's Ian Danoff!"

Dani and Winn came toward Ian. "Marvellous!" Dani exclaimed, giving him a big kiss. "That is absolutely fabulous! What gave you the idea?"

Ian was grinning so hard his face hurt. "It was nothing," he said happily. "Just a little gag I dreamed up."

Winn was also grinning. "I've never seen anyone more spooked than the bunch of us at the campfire when the music came out of the night. We were frozen solid. You'll go down in camp history for this."

"Sounds pretty good," Ian said. "In fact, nothing could sound better!"

* * *

Late in the night, Parrish finally crawled into his sleeping bag. Earlier he'd unrolled it far from the fire, so he could slip away without the other counsellors knowing. Now he looked at his watch, shook his head in dismay at the hour, and tried to sleep.

But his mind was spinning with fears. Not just of Clay Croxley discovering his secret, but also his fears about the person he cared for so deeply. He sensed something was wrong, and a crisis was just ahead. But how could he prevent the worst happening?

Finally he fell into an unhappy sleep. Once he awoke to see yellow and orange layers of dawn, then returned to dreams until a hand shook him awake.

"Hey, *monsieur le chef*," Linda said. "Rise and shine, if you're going to cook all those omelettes."

Parrish groaned, remembering his foolish promise to cook breakfast. He sat up, feeling every bone creak, and looked at the tall grass bending under the wind. The prairie was so beautiful. The lake glistened with sunlight, wispy clouds were high in the blue sky, and birds played everywhere.

At the tent, the boys were in great spirits. Ian was everyone's hero for his spectacular gag, and his face was shining. As the boy pulled on a T-shirt, Parrish noticed that his back was a criss-cross of scars from operations. For a moment he felt sorry for the pain Ian had suffered in life, but his own aching heart reminded him that the boy wasn't alone.

"Are you guys ready for the breakfast to end breakfasts? My omelettes will have your stomachs crying for more."

"Hey Parrish," Corny shouted, "if you're going to be a teacher, tell me which is correct. The yolk of an egg is white, or the yolk of an egg are white?"

"I'm no fool, Corny. Obviously the yolk of an egg is white."

The boy crowed with delight. "No, it isn't! The yolk's yellow."

As Parrish groaned, Ian gave Corny an affectionate bear hug. "My buddy's got the world's largest collection of jokes, all squeezed inside that pointy little head. I think I'll be his manager, and put him on tour. I'll clean up."

"No!" Corny protested. "*We'll* clean up."

"Right on!"

Before long they were all out of the tent except Ken, who was battling to get his arms into an Hawaiian shirt with a mind-blowing design. Leaving Ken to his struggles, Parrish headed for the firepit. Soon a collection of kids were watching the first of his cheese omelettes turn golden brown in a buttered frying pan.

"Hey, Parrish," Ian said, "Why is this lake called Little Manitou?"

"The Indians named it for Manitou, their greatest god. When a war ended between two tribes, they'd come here to make peace and forgive each other. They also called it the Lake of Healing Waters, which I think is nice."

"How do you know all that?"

Parrish shrugged, keeping his eyes on the frying pan. "It's pretty common knowledge. Everyone in Saskatchewan has heard the story of Little Manitou Lake."

"I doubt it." Ian waited until Parrish glanced his way. There was a smile on the boy's face. "You do know a lot about this area."

Parrish tried to hold Ian's eyes, but failed. Sliding the omelette onto a paper plate, he turned to Tracy. "Ladies first."

"Chauvinist!" the girl's tiny voice whispered. "Give it to Ian. He was here ahead of me."

Ian reached for the plate, grinning. "I won't argue. When a person's been up half the night, it gives him an appetite." His eyes betrayed nothing as he said this, but Parrish suspected Ian knew a lot.

He glanced at Winn, who sat nearby buttering bread. "Want some help? You must be getting frustrated."

"I am! This is a tough job."

"Rico could lend a hand."

"Forget it, Parrish! I need to do this." The dark eyes in Winn's handsome face never wavered as he fought to make his toes control a knife that was slippery with butter. Little of the bread was ready to eat, but the campers didn't seem to mind.

A horn sounded from the hillside as the bus approached. Blondie got out, waving happily. Soon she'd heard all about the mysterious voice singing hymns in the night, and was looking at Ian with adoring eyes. Parrish smiled.

"Ian should get the Order of Canada. Talk about bravery."

"That's the medal they gave Terry Fox. No way I'm like him."

"You never know, Ian. People can have their own style of courage."

Greyeyes looked up from his plate. "I want to be a star like Terry Fox," he said, his mouth full.

"I'll probably play pro baseball."

"How?" Corny said. "You can't even use that arm of yours."

"Ever heard of Pete Gray?"

"Nope."

"He had one arm, but he played pro ball for St. Louis. If he could do it, so can I. Our names are practically the same."

"Good luck with it," Corny said. "Me, I'm going on the rubber-chicken circuit, knocking 'em dead with my yuks. Just ask my manager."

Ian grinned. "My boy Corny is a champion. So is Greyeyes. I've been out with him while he trained for the big relay."

"Hey!" Susanna exclaimed. "That's today. We'd better get home."

"Finish your omelette," Parrish ordered sternly. "There are starving children who'd give anything to have it."

She giggled. "Especially if it came complete with the chef."

Tracy nodded. "Are you ever going to get married, Parrish?"

He shrugged, pretending not to notice that Dani's blue eyes had suddenly looked his way. "Who knows? Maybe I'll marry you, Tracy."

"Wow!" she said, grinning.

Susanna looked at Parrish with a determined face. "I want to have a bunch of kids. I already asked the doctor and she said it's possible, even if I am in a wheelchair. Am I ever going to love those little devils."

"How about you, Tracy? Got any plans?"

"University," she whispered. "It's going to be tough, but I can do it. I've already planned the courses for a career in pharmacy. I need top marks, because I'm going to be competing for a job with able-bodied people." She sighed. "With you by my side I could conquer the world."

Parrish blushed, and everyone laughed.

Rico wheeled closer to the fire. "I'd love to be a rock singer but I'm too lazy. So I'm going to be a disc jockey. Before long you'll hear me on your all-night radio, burning up the airwaves. *Hey, cool folks, it's your main man spinning the platters for all you lonely listeners while the coyotes howl under the Northern Lights and hearts get broken by those lying eyes.*" He grinned. "How's that sound?"

"You're hired!" Speedball exclaimed.

"I'm thinking of being a writer," Ian said quietly, "but I don't know. Maybe it's a dumb idea."

"I want . . . to be . . . a . . . magician." Ken took out his deck of cards. With enormous concentration, he forced his spastic hands to open the package. The cards appeared, shining brightly in the sun, and were spread in a fan. "Some . . . one . . ."

Suddenly his muscles lost control. The cards scattered in the dirt at his feet, and he looked at them with unhappy eyes. Then he knelt down to begin collecting them.

"Okay, gang," Parrish said, "time to clean up the camp site, then we'll head home to watch Greyeyes star in the relay."

Greyeyes leapt to his feet to perform a victory dance. "I am so beautiful. I am such a champion. I will whip the world."

Parrish laughed. "Let's hope so, kiddo."

NINE

A large crowd of people from nearby communities had gathered for the relay at Manitou Beach, a collection of brightly painted beach houses and stores spread along the lake close to Camp Easter Seal. Besides teams from the camp and Watrous, there were entries in the relay from the towns of Lanigan, Drake and Allan.

Parrish pushed his way through the crowd carrying ice cream to Linda and the others, who stood between the main road and the hot sands of the beach. "Everyone's saying Lanigan is pretty powerful this year."

"We'll take it again," Ian said. "My boy Greyeyes is a fantastic runner. He can't be beaten."

Ken turned to Winn. "How ... does ... the ... relay ... work?"

"There are eight sections. The relay starts with a three-legged race from the gates of our camp, but that section's too far away for us to see. Then each team passes its baton to a bicycle rider."

"Where ... do ... the ... bikes ... race?"

"Along this road. They'll go right past us, then disappear around that bend. Greyeyes and the other foot racers will take over, then the batons will be passed to people in canoes, more runners and finally swimmers. The team with the first swimmer to reach this beach wins the relay."

"It's started!" someone shouted. The crowd pressed close to the road, hoping foolishly they could see the three-legged racers. Within seconds rumours began to buzz.

"Watrous is winning!" a young woman said, giving her baby a happy kiss. "Come on, team! Come on!"

Parrish stared down the road, wondering

where she got her information. "Come on, Camp Easter Seal!" he cried. "We're number one!" The others joined in, and the crowd was making an enormous racket when a group of racers swept past on their bicycles, muscles straining.

"We're winning!" Linda shouted, as they disappeared down the road. "We're winning!"

The bicycles had been bunched so tightly together that Parrish hadn't even seen the camp racer, but he was obviously doing well. Now came the scary part, for the batons would be passed to the runners. How would Greyeyes do?

"When will the runners get here?" Ian asked Winn.

"We won't see them."

"What! Why not?"

"We can't see their section of the relay from here. Then they'll pass the batons to people in canoes."

"But we won't know who was the best runner!"

Winn looked toward a point of land, jutting into the lake. "When the canoes appear from behind that point, we'll know who won the running section. If our canoe is first, we'll know it was Greyeyes."

Again, rumours spread through the crowd as people anxiously watched the lake. Someone shouted that Lanigan was so far ahead that the other teams had quit. This was greeted by some laughter, but the tension quickly returned.

Suddenly a canoe appeared from behind the point. Parrish's heart skipped, then he felt overwhelming disappointment when he realized it wasn't the camp canoe. A second canoe appeared, and a third, but there was no sign of the camp's paddler.

"Where is he?" Linda said anxiously.

"At last!" Parrish shouted. "Come on, Don!"

The camp's green canoe pulled into sight, the

counsellor in its stern fighting to cut the gap. His paddle stroked cleanly through the water and slowly he closed the distance as the canoes raced toward the far shore, then landed one by one.

Straining his eyes, Parrish watched a runner start up the hill. Even from this distance, it was obvious that he was having trouble getting a footing on the steep hillside. By now the other paddlers had passed batons to their runners, who set off in pursuit.

"Which ... one ... is ours?" Ken asked.

"The girl in the green T-shirt, and I think she's gaining!"

The lead runner was having a terrible time, slipping and sliding on the rocky slope. As he struggled upward, the Camp Easter Seal runner and another person were climbing remorselessly. A minute later, all three reached the top together.

Batons were passed, and three more figures started down, dust flying from their feet as they scrambled and ran and leapt down the slope. Their progress was watched intently by a new set of paddlers, who were waiting in the canoes to receive the batons.

A cloud of dust rose as one runner fell, twisting and tumbling to a stop. The crowd held its breath, then relaxed when he stood up to rejoin the race. Meanwhile the others had reached the bottom, and two canoes pulled into the lake.

"We're winning!" Winn yelled.

Sunshine flashed from the paddles rising and falling, rising and falling. The crowd roared its encouragement as the canoes raced toward a barge anchored in the lake. On it, swimmers from each team waited to break for shore, and victory.

"Come on!" Ian screamed, then looked at Winn. "What team is the other canoe?"

"Lanigan."

"Oh, no!"

At the barge the camp's swimming instructor, Kathy McMaster, balanced on the railing as she waited to dive into the lake. Beside her was a teenage boy with something like a thousand muscles bulging under his brown skin.

The green canoe from Camp Easter Seal was the first to reach the barge. Kathy's body arced out in a low dive, and she was stroking steadily toward the beach when the teenager hit the water. Using a powerful crawl, he set out at an angle which put him on a collision course with Kathy.

"They're going to hit!" Winn shouted. "Why doesn't he watch out?"

"Turn, you idiot!" Ian shouted. "Turn!"

The teenager kept his face below the surface, except for turning up for air, and it wasn't clear if he saw Kathy. The crowd screamed in warning, but he went straight at her like a torpedo. They collided in a flurry of arms and legs, then the teenager continued toward shore as Kathy struggled to regain her form. Within a minute, the boy from Lanigan splashed to the beach in triumph, and his supporters went crazy.

Turning, the victor gallantly lifted Kathy's arm into the air when she reached the beach. The crowd applauded enthusiastically, but Kathy seemed ready to cry as a towel was wrapped around her shoulders.

"We were robbed!" Ian's voice was rough from shouting. "Kathy would have won if that bruiser hadn't mowed her down."

"I don't know," Parrish said. "I think he would have taken it anyway. He's a great swimmer."

"It was sabotage!"

"Take it easy, Ian. We won last year, and now it's Lanigan's turn."

The camp pickup truck pulled up nearby. Inside were Clay Croxley, Greyeyes, and the team's cyclist. As they walked slowly toward the others, defeat and despair marked Greyeyes' face.

"Here's our man!" Parrish said cheerfully. "How about a Coke, Greyeyes? You've earned it."

Shaking his head, he sat down and turned his face away from the others.

"I'm very proud of Greyeyes," Clay said. "He did tremendously against runners who were older and stronger."

"That's our boy!" Winn said.

Greyeyes shifted unhappily, his eyes on the ground. "I let down the team," he said miserably.

Linda sat beside him. "You won the try-outs, which means you're the best runner in camp. Next year you'll do even better."

"I can't wait!" Ian exclaimed, wheeling over to put an arm around Greyeyes. Moved by the compassion in Ian's gesture, Parrish left them alone and headed for the food stand. To his pleasure, Dani was also there.

"How's Greyeyes feeling?" she asked.

"Pretty rough, but he'll be okay."

"Parrish, I ..." She paused. "I, well, I was in the office at camp and happened to see the list of counsellors' T.O. Did you know we're both off at three this afternoon?"

"That sounds kind of interesting."

"Our girls are staying here to have lunch and later go swimming. I wonder if, maybe, you'd meet me here at three? We could spend some time together."

Parrish grinned happily. "It's a date." Feeling marvellous, he bought treats for everyone in his cabin, and ate a Giant Cone hungrily as they headed back to camp.

Unfortunately, Greyeyes remained very depressed. He couldn't eat any lunch, then asked to lie down instead of participating in the afternoon horseshoe tournament. Parrish watched him leave for the cabin, head hanging, and felt sad.

"Greyeyes is taking it worse than I expected," he said to Linda. "I'd like to talk to him."

"No problem. Winn and I can take the kids to horseshoes."

At the cabin, Parrish found Greyeyes crying on his bed. The boy tried to hide his face, but Parrish sat down beside him. "Hey, it's okay to cry. I know you feel rotten."

Greyeyes tried to push him away, then let his misery flow. Deep sobs shook his body until finally he was exhausted. Then he turned his face to the wall. "I let down the team. It's my fault we lost."

"You won the try-outs. Nobody from our camp could have done better."

"I should have done more training. My coach says I'm too lazy."

"I'm sure you'll start to train, now you know how important it is."

Greyeyes sighed deeply. "Everyone in camp is going to hate me."

Parrish smiled. "Why's that?"

"They expected me to win."

"No, Greyeyes. They expected you to give your very best. Isn't that what happened?"

He shrugged.

"Clay Croxley saw you run. He said he's proud of you."

"He's just being nice."

For a long time Greyeyes was silent, then

drifted into sleep. Parrish continued to sit beside him, feeling his presence was a comfort. Finally the boy woke up, and smiled faintly. "Thanks for being here."

"You want to be alone now?"

"No."

Parrish glanced at his watch. Already it was 2:45 p.m., and it took fifteen minutes to walk to the beach. "You seem pretty relaxed now, champ. How about going to the horseshoe tournament? I'm sure you'll clean up on the trophies."

"I'm still sad, Parrish, but being with you makes me feel better."

Parrish thought about walking along the sand with Dani. He knew he'd feel good, just being with her, and he desperately needed someone to talk to. But so did Greyeyes.

"Say, champ, do you like canoes?"

"I've never been in one."

"How about if we go for a paddle? I'll tell you about some basketball games my team has lost because of my mistakes. I've missed some training sessions, too."

Greyeyes jumped up, his eyes sparkling. "This is going to be fun!"

"You bet," Parrish said, glancing at his watch a final time as he put away all thoughts of Dani.

TEN

The next day, Ian sat on the dock, filled with panic, as he watched Parrish and Linda put paddles into the camp canoes and collect life jackets.

He was terrified of water. All his life he'd had nightmares in which he sank below the surface of a great body of water, and could do nothing. In the dreams, his arms thrashed and struggled, trying to carry his body to the surface, but his legs did nothing. He screamed to his legs *save me!* but they remained lifeless.

So he sank, down and down, beneath the cold, uncaring weight of the water.

Sweat stood on Ian's face as he remembered those nightmares. He looked at the grey waves moving restlessly under a strong wind, then reached for the wheels of his chair. He had to get away, he had to escape. But his hands refused to obey.

"Okay, guys!" Linda said cheerfully. "Who's first?"

"Not me," Corny replied. "Canoes tip. I'm too young to drown."

Greyeyes held up his hand. "I'll go! Parrish and I had a great time on the lake yesterday."

Parrish smiled. "That's right, so you should let someone else go first. Ian, how about you?"

Ian opened his mouth, but he couldn't speak. Slowly he shook his head, keeping his eyes on the rough planks of the dock.

"You can do it, buddy." Parrish grabbed a life jacket and put Ian's hands through the loops. Ian wanted to struggle, but he was too numb to move. The life jacket in place, Parrish pushed his wheelchair to the side of the dock where a canoe was waiting. His body dead, Ian allowed himself to be lifted from the wheelchair into the stern.

"I want you in charge of this canoe, so you're in the stern. You'll learn to paddle, you'll learn to steer, you'll be in complete control. I know you can do it, Ian."

As Parrish stepped into the bow, the canoe wobbled dangerously. With sightless eyes, Ian watched Parrish push away from the dock and begin paddling. Within minutes, the canoe was all alone, far from shore.

"Come on, Ian!" Parrish said. "Put those muscles to work."

Ian didn't move. His hands gripped the canoe so tightly that they were white.

Parrish looked back over his shoulder. "What's the problem?"

Ian could only stare.

"Are you scared?"

For a long moment, nothing happened. Then Ian nodded.

"Do you want to turn back?"

"Yes," Ian whispered.

"Then reach for that paddle, and turn the canoe around."

"You do it. Please, Parrish."

He shook his head. "No chance. Ian, I know how frightened you felt on the dock. That's why I forced you to come out here. But I can't keep making the decisions for you. From now on, it's up to you. You can stay out here, or you can paddle the canoe back to the dock. Either way, you'll be the one who makes the decision."

Ian stared at him miserably. "Why are you being so mean?"

"I'm not, Ian. I care for you a lot more than you know. That's why I want you to learn today there's real strength inside you. What you did at the ghost camp was marvellous — now be a man again."

Ian continued to stare at Parrish's blue eyes, then looked down at the paddle. "I don't know how to work that thing."

"Just lift it up." Parrish waited. "That's good. Now, grip the end in one hand, and the middle in the other."

With great hesitation, Ian dipped the paddle into the water. A shock of fear ran through him as the canoe wobbled, then he gave a tentative thrust and felt it move forward.

"Good man, Ian. Now paddle on the other side."

After several minutes of paddling, Ian grinned. "Hey, this is easy!"

In the distance, the shape of the waves changed. They seemed to flatten for a moment, then leapt higher. White spray flew. Something changed about the wind on Ian's face, and fear returned.

"Parrish, look at the lake!"

"It's okay, Ian, we can ride it out."

"I'm scared!"

Putting his paddle across the canoe, Parrish waited calmly for the squall to hit. But panic overwhelmed Ian, and he lashed at the water with his paddle. The canoe tilted just as the wind hit. For a moment there was nothing but fear, and then there was nothing but nightmare.

As Ian screamed, water buried him. He thrashed his arms, but they were pressed by a great weight. Then he knew nothing until air was on his face, and he was crying, and he was spitting water from his mouth.

"It's okay," Parrish's voice said. His strong hands gripped Ian. "You're safe. Just relax. The canoe tipped over, and we're in the water, but we won't drown. You have your life jacket on. The motorboat will be coming to help. Just float on the surface until it gets here."

Slowly the fear died, was replaced by a time of calmness, and then by anger. He had trusted Parrish, and been betrayed. His nightmares had come true, and all because of Parrish. Terrible thoughts filled Ian as he heard the sound of the motorboat, then felt himself being lifted from the lake and wrapped in a blanket. Words were spoken, but they meant nothing. People looked into his face, but they had become strangers.

Ian could do nothing but hate.

Parrish came to kneel beside him. "It's too bad about the accident, Ian, but no harm done. You were handling the canoe well until the squall hit."

"I panicked."

"That's right, but it doesn't matter. So we got soaked — big deal."

"Did you tell those people it was my fault?"

"Of course not."

"I bet you did!" Ian said angrily. "I bet you told them about your big plans to make me courageous. Those plans always flop, Parrish, and I end up looking like a fool!"

"Hey, hey, calm down. It wasn't important that the canoe tipped. It happens all the time."

"Not to me. I feel humiliated *again*."

"I'd better leave you alone, Ian. You'll feel better soon."

"I doubt it," he said bitterly, watching the counsellor move to the bow of the motorboat. When it reached the dock people crowded around, asking a million questions, wanting to know what had caused the accident. Ian ignored everyone, and was desperately thankful that Linda, not Parrish, was the person who wheeled him to the cabin for a change of clothes.

For the rest of the day, Ian raged. He was unable to eat the evening meal, and sat with a frozen face during campfire. His only thoughts were of the counsellor's betrayal, and how that could be avenged.

Then, like a miracle, he got his chance.

After campfire he was waiting for Linda to accompany him to the cabin when a young man approached. Putting his arms around Linda he gave her a big hug. They spoke briefly, laughing happily, before she introduced Ian. "I'd like you to meet my brother, Tyler. He's paying me a surprise visit."

"Pleased to meet you," Ian said, shaking hands.

"The other boys have already gone to the cabin, Tyler, but you can meet them tomorrow." Linda turned to Ian. "We're going into Watrous for a coffee. Tell Parrish he owes me an evening time off, and I'm collecting! I'll be back later."

Ian watched them go, unable to believe his luck. Humming a tune, he wheeled closer to the dying embers of the fire as he considered his strategy.

Shortly after, Parrish came to the campfire circle. "Why hasn't Linda brought you to the cabin, Ian?"

"She had to visit the biffy in a big hurry, but she left you a message."

"Oh? What's that?"

"You can have her evening T.O."

"But I've already taken one of hers."

"She said she's not feeling well. She just feels like lying down this evening, so there's no reason for both of you to be in the cabin. She said you can take off as soon as everyone's in bed."

A look of great relief crossed Parrish's face. His spirits seemed to improve, and he chatted happily to Ian as they returned to the cabin.

Once there, however, he seemed to sag again. Something was definitely troubling the counsellor but Ian didn't care about that. He just watched Parrish carefully and, shortly after the nurses had made their visit to the cabin, was delighted to see him leave.

"Where's Parrish gone?" Rico said into the darkness. "We've never been alone at night before."

Ian faked a noisy yawn. "He's probably gone to the biffy. Get some sleep, Rico."

"We'll ... be ... okay," Ken said. "Linda ... will ... be ... here ... soon."

Corny spoke next, and he sounded frightened. "Sometimes I have seizures. There's supposed to be a counsellor here in case that happens. Someone has to help me, or I can hurt myself really bad."

Ian felt his face turning warm. "It's okay, Corny. If anything happens, I'll go for help."

"That'll be too late! I'm scared, Ian. Why isn't someone here?"

A noise came from Ken's direction. Ian knew he was struggling to get up and go for help. He hadn't expected this. His strategy was turning out to be full of holes, but if he could keep the others calm, just until Clay Croxley made his rounds and discovered that Parrish had abandoned the cabin, his revenge would be complete.

Ian sat up. "I'll go find another counsellor. Corny, can you just relax for now? You haven't had a seizure since coming to camp."

"I know, Ian. They don't happen very often, but I get them when I'm scared."

"Then don't be scared." After dressing, Ian wheeled across to his friend's bed. Large eyes looked up at him. "I'm going for help, and I'll be back shortly."

"Will you hurry?"

"Sure."

Ian continued to sit beside Corny until his breathing became more regular. "Are you feeling better?" he whispered.

"A bit."

"Think you can sleep?"

"Maybe. That pill the nurses give me every night usually puts me out."

"Then just relax, and I'll find someone."

Going outside, Ian left the door open a crack to listen for conversation. Nobody said anything more, and he even thought he heard faint snoring, but time was limited. Then he saw Winn approaching. Seizing the wheels of his chair, Ian powered along the ramp toward him. "Hi there!" he said, trying to sound cheerful.

"Why are you up, Ian?"

"Just heading for the biffy. What are you doing?"

"I'm going to the cabin with a message for Parrish."

"Why don't I take it to him?"

"Sure. Clay Croxley wants to see him first thing in the morning."

A wave of guilt swept over Ian. By the morning Parrish would be out of a job. He struggled to feel good about this, then held out a hand as Winn turned to leave.

"What's the matter? Is something wrong?"

Ian looked up at the night. Usually there were stars, but tonight the sky was stormy. "What do you think of Parrish?"

"I admire him enormously. He's the kind of counsellor I want to be."

"Why?"

"He cares so much for people. He puts his whole heart into this camp."

"But half the time he zombies around."

"Well, he's got a tough job. It's physically

demanding, which is a real drain on a person."

"But ..." Ian gazed in the direction of the dark lake, feeling miserable. "But, the first time at the ghost camp he got me into the building so I could look like a fool."

"I told you that stunt was my idea, Ian. In fact, before camp started I got Linda's permission to tell you guys that fake legend. My counsellors fed us the same line a couple of years ago. It's all supposed to be fun."

"*Fake legend?*" Ian stared at him, shocked. "You mean it's not true? You never heard children singing hymns?"

Winn laughed. "Well, I imagined hearing them."

For several minutes Ian sat silently, looking at the dark outline of the lake. "I guess I haven't been completely fair to Parrish. But then we had that arm wrestle in the restaurant. He destroyed me."

"You hadn't done anything wrong?"

Ian blushed, remembering how he'd mocked Corny in order to hide his own fears. "Well, maybe," he mumbled. "But today out on the lake, Parrish played me for a fool and I got soaked."

"You ..."

"I know," Ian said, raising a hand. "You don't have to tell me. I was the one who panicked when the big waves were coming." He sighed deeply. "I always figured Parrish didn't like me, because he kept hurting my feelings."

"You want to know something I learned from my best friend? When a person is hurting your feelings, tell him it's hurting and ask him to stop. If he cares for you, he'll stop. If he keeps on hurting you, then he never cared, anyway."

Ian thought about this. "Yeah," he said at last.

"I guess that's what I should have done with Parrish."

"It's never too late. Why don't you go back to the cabin now, and talk."

Like a jolt of electricity, the memory of what he'd done returned to Ian. Quickly, he looked at his watch, then at Winn. "Thanks for straightening me out."

Winn laughed. "I'll see you tomorrow, Ian."

He disappeared into the night. Again Ian looked at his watch, then made a decision. Wheeling to the end of the ramp, he turned on to the gravel road that led to the lake. It took a lot of effort to force his chair over rocks and through ruts, and before long his face was covered with sweat.

At the dock waves lapped around the pilings, driven by an unseen wind. Somewhere over the dark waters a bird cried, and was answered by another. The dock creaked as Ian wheeled out. The only boats there were the canoes, rising and falling on the waves.

He put on a life jacket. Then he released a canoe from its mooring at the bow, and wheeled to the stern. Getting down from his chair, he lowered himself into the canoe, picked up a paddle and reached for the rope which held the canoe to the dock.

Ian hesitated, overwhelmed by fear of the water.

Then he released the rope, and paddled out into the darkness. Waves slapped and banged against the canoe's thin sides, threatening to flip it, but Ian remembered the paddling lesson he'd received from Parrish and kept it under control. Then the wind rose up, and fear pounded inside his heart as the lights of the camp were left behind.

But still he drove the canoe forward.

At last, with his body overwhelmed by exhaustion, Ian neared his goal. Turning the canoe closer to land, he looked up the hillside at the outlined shapes of the ghost camp buildings. Still he kept paddling, until another building was in sight.

Then he ran the canoe up on shore, feeling it grind over the pebbles and rocks. Manoeuvering forward to the bow, Ian lowered himself to the rough stones of the beach and heaved his way across it.

Finally, he reached the cabin.

A light shone faintly from a window, but there were no sounds. Ian hesitated outside the door, wondering if he'd made a terrible mistake.

Then he knocked.

There was no answer so he tried again, louder this time. When still no sound was heard from behind the door, he pushed it open. Light spilled into his eyes, blinding him for a moment, and then he saw Parrish. There were tears in the counsellor's eyes.

On the floor lay a woman.

ELEVEN

She was elderly. Ian was surprised at how much grey hair she had, thick on her head and spread around her shoulders. Her wrinkled face was absolutely white, and glistened with moisture. She lay on her back, unmoving, with her eyes closed.

"Ian!" Parrish exclaimed. "Thank God! You've got to help."

Without saying anything, Ian pulled himself across the floor. Although his attention was focused on Parrish, he was aware of feminine surroundings: dresses in an open closet, a nightgown folded on the bed, in the air a sweet smell he associated with his mother.

"Who is she, Parrish?"

For a moment he didn't reply. He leaned close to the woman, listening for breathing, then reached for her arms, which were folded across her chest. He pressed down, then pulled up.

"She's my grandmother, Ian. She's lived in this cabin most of her life. A month ago she had a heart attack, but refused to leave here. She says she's going to die in this cabin, but I can't let that happen." He turned to Ian. The tears were running down his face. "I've been checking on her every night. I knew something was going wrong, and tonight it happened. She had another attack, but I got here in time. I've been keeping her alive and praying for a miracle."

"What should I do?"

"Watch how I do this, then take over. I need to get to the farm over the hill to phone for an ambulance."

A few minutes later, Ian was alone with the woman. Although he was afraid she might die, he did his best to follow the instructions Parrish had given. Somewhere in the cabin a clock ticked, then it announced the hour with chimes, but Ian continued to use his strong arms to give life to Parrish's grandmother.

At last the door crashed open. "Is she okay?" Parrish said, breathing hard from his long run.

"She's the same. Is an ambulance coming?"

"Yes, but it will be a while. Let me take over." He knelt down beside his grandmother, checked her breathing, then looked at Ian. "Why'd you come here tonight?"

"There was a reason, but I can't talk about it now. It's more important that I get back to camp, and fast."

Parrish smiled unhappily. "I'd almost forgotten about camp. It was a great place."

"It still is."

Parrish shook his head. "Not for me."

* * *

The cabin was silent. Ian wheeled in the door, his body numb with exhaustion, and sat for a moment without moving. Corny was mumbling in a dream, and the others were also asleep, but what about Linda? Ian carefully pulled back the blanket which covered her corner of the cabin and was relieved to see she hadn't yet returned.

Crossing quickly to Parrish's bed, he went to work. Within minutes he'd used a blanket and some pillows to make a dummy. Wheeling away from the bed, Ian studied the dummy and decided that — in the dim light — it looked exactly like a sleeping figure.

Very soon he was in bed, but not asleep. Eventually Linda tip-toed into the cabin, checked each boy, and went to bed. Soon after, the sound of her breathing told Ian she was asleep.

He checked his watch. Clay Croxley was late for his patrol, but surely he'd still be here. Ian shifted his body, trying to get comfortable as he stared at the ceiling. Then his eyes went to the door.

Someone was coming.

The footsteps paused outside, and the person coughed. Parrish or Clay? Ian's concentration on the door was total. It opened, and Clay Croxley entered. He went quietly to each boy, glancing toward Parrish's bed, then went out.

"Wow!" Ian breathed quietly to himself. "It worked!"

Now all that remained was to pray that Clay didn't spot Parrish returning from his grandmother's cabin. As time passed Ian relaxed, and was drifting into a pleasant sleep when he heard the door open again. He glanced over, expecting to see Parrish, and got a terrible shock.

Clay Croxley had returned.

The man crossed straight to Parrish's bed, switched on a flashlight, and lifted away the bedclothes. One of the pillows tumbled to the floor. Ian held his breath. Then he sat up.

"Clay!" he called softly. "May I speak to you?"

The man came to his bed. "Why aren't you asleep?"

"Is Parrish in trouble?"

"It's not your problem, Ian. Now try to get some sleep."

Ian's mind was in turmoil as he watched Clay walk away. He tried to believe Parrish deserved everything that would happen, tried to believe he shouldn't get involved.

"Clay! Please come back."

Once again the man came to the bed. "Yes?"

"Clay ..."

"What is it, Ian?"

Ian's heart was pounding terribly, but he managed to look straight at the man. "It's my fault. I'm the one who made that dummy. I'm the one who tried to get Parrish into trouble."

"Perhaps you'd better tell me about it."

Ian sighed deeply, then told his story. It required strength to tell it all, and to tell it honestly, because Clay's black eyes never left his face, and the man never said a word. Finally, when it was over, Clay squeezed Ian's hand. "Thank you," he said quietly. "That took courage." Then he left the cabin, and Ian was left feeling dismal.

* * *

In the morning, Parrish reported to Clay's office. The door was closed, so he waited outside feeling more nervous than ever before in his life. Very shortly he would know if he was staying at Camp Easter Seal, or being fired.

At last the door opened. To his surprise, Ian rolled out in his wheelchair. The boy gave him a strange look, then left. At the same moment, Clay appeared at the door. "Hello there, Parrish," he said. As usual, his voice and face revealed nothing. "There's been a delay. Can we talk this evening, just before campfire?"

Parrish nodded, trying to hide his disappointment. He'd steeled his nerves for this moment, and now he had to wait. As a result, the morning passed very slowly, but he'd made special arrangements for his afternoon T.O., and that was something to think about.

By three o'clock he was on the road to Watrous, driving a borrowed car. Beside him sat Ian. So far they hadn't said much, preferring to concentrate on the prairie sky. It was an amazing colour, deep and shimmering, its beauty matched by the vivid greens of the young wheat bending under the wind.

"I love Saskatchewan," Parrish said. "This will always be my home, no matter where I live."

"Parrish, I'm sorry."

He smiled. "What for? That I love Saskatchewan?"

"About all the things I've done." Ian's face was red. "About not liking you after what happened at the ghost camp, and ... wrecking your career as a counsellor."

"How ...?" Parrish said, then bit back the question. Instead he gave Ian a friendly punch on the shoulder. "It's my fault, too. We can't change what happened, Ian, but we started talking in enough time to still be friends."

"I'm glad of that."

For a while they were silent, watching the fields roll past. Then Parrish spoke. "I liked it when you named our cabin for Terry Fox. What do you think of him?"

"He's my number one hero. I've read that book about him a bunch of times." Ian hesitated. "But he depresses me, too."

"How so?"

"Because he was so strong, and he accomplished so much. I could never be like that."

Parrish smiled. "Not even after last night?"

"That was different. I just paddled to your grandmother's place."

"It didn't take courage?"

Ian shrugged. "I don't know. I hadn't thought about it."

"That's because it happened to you personally. I bet that the whole time Terry Fox was running he just felt like an ordinary person, doing his best."

"Do you think I've got the guts to stand up to my parents?"

"Why do you ask?"

"Because tomorrow I'm going home, and they're always protecting me. They want to get a power wheelchair, and they send me to a special school so I won't get teased. I want to go to an ordinary school. It's hard to be a kid when all the decisions are made for you."

"Know what I'd do?" Parrish paused, thinking. "Tomorrow I'd tell them again why I don't want a power wheelchair. Then, if they insisted on buying one, I wouldn't use it. No one can force you to sit in the thing, or push the levers to make it run."

"But what about the school?"

"Explain why you don't want to go. Let them know how important it is that you attend your neighbourhood school." Parrish smiled. "I've got problems with my parents, too. They expect me to take over our family's department store in Regina. I keep saying I'm going to be a teacher, and they keep blowing their tops, and I keep repeating I'll be a teacher, anyway. Even if they don't like what I'm saying, I know they respect me."

"Where do you get that strength from?"

Parrish laughed. "Probably my grandmother. She practically raised me when I was a kid, because my parents were going through problems with their marriage. She's a very wise person, and stubborn. Nobody can force her to do anything. When she had her first heart attack my parents demanded that she move into a rest home, but she'd never leave her cabin because of other people's fears for her safety. That got my parents so angry they've been ignoring her, and that's one reason why I applied for this job at camp. Every night I've gone down the lake to be sure she's okay, and to give her some company. The last few nights I was really worried, because her health seemed weaker, but she refused to move into town to be closer to a doctor."

"It's interesting, Parrish, how I used to think you didn't have a care in the world. How wrong I was."

"Problems are a part of everyone's life. What makes the difference is how we handle them."

"I guess you knew the location of the Pool Hall, and the history of this area, from living here with your grandmother?"

"You got it. Ever thought of being a detective?"

Ian laughed. "Nope."

"I'll always be grateful for what you did last night. It was a miracle when you came through the door, and I'd never believed in miracles before."

"Faith can move mountains." Ian smiled. "I've got a Granny too, and that's what she says when I get blue about being in a wheelchair."

"You may never walk, Ian, but I know you'll accomplish a lot in life."

"You know something? After what I did last night, I believe it. This camp has made me feel really good about myself. Just watch me now — soon I'll be wheeling to our local school in my stripped-down racing chair!"

Parrish gave his hand a brief, hard squeeze. "Good man."

Nothing more was said, and soon they reached Watrous. They parked at the hospital, a large building on the edge of town, and took the elevator to the top floor. After a long delay, Parrish met his grandmother's doctor before being taken to see her. She was inside an oxygen tent, sleeping, so he was only able to sit at the bedside, holding her hand. Then he went to the waiting room for Ian, and together they drove back to camp.

Soon after, the time came for his meeting with Clay Croxley. Parrish walked into his office on trembling legs. "Sit down, please," Clay said, gesturing at a chair. He looked at some papers on his desk, then turned his black eyes to Parrish.

"How's your grandmother?"

"She's a little better." Parrish was unable to hide his surprise. "How did you know?"

"My ear is usually pretty close to the ground, Parrish. I admit, however, that I only learned about your grandmother very recently." Again he consulted the papers in front of him. "Made any plans for the rest of the summer?"

Parrish's heart sank. "No, sir," he mumbled.

"What about your family's department store? Can't you work there?"

"Sure, but I won't. They'd only think I'm weakening about having a career at the store."

"I see." Clay picked up one of the papers. "Parrish, I've made some notes about your work as a counsellor. You've made a lot of mistakes. That episode in the canoe with Ian was the worst — you shouldn't have done that."

Parrish waited silently. His face was numb.

"Should I run through the rest of my list?"

"No, sir. I think I'd probably know it by heart."

"Then I'd like you to look at something." Clay handed him a sheet of paper. *Petition* it said at the top. *We the undersigned* ...

Parrish's eyes skimmed down it. "I don't understand."

"Ian Danoff brought that petition to me this morning. All the boys in your cabin signed it, Parrish. They want you to keep your job as counsellor. Ian was here a long time, telling me why."

Parrish shook his head. "They're a great bunch."

"The petition didn't change my mind, but it was certainly a nice gesture." Clay paused. "When Ian arrived with it, I'd already decided to offer you a permanent job."

"What?"

Clay smiled. "My opinion of you began to

change after the relay. Instead of meeting Dani at the beach, you spent your time with Greyeyes."

"How'd you know ...?"

Clay laughed, then held out his hand. "Welcome to the permanent staff, Parrish. You've got a very bright future at Camp Easter Seal."

"Wow!" Parrish exclaimed, leaping up from his chair. "I can't believe it!" Quickly he shook Clay's hand, then raced from the office. Minutes later he found Dani, whose face shone as he gave the news.

"So," he said finally. "I can go to your family reunion as long as there's no change in my grandmother's condition."

"Great!"

Parrish grinned. "This is the best day of my life."

EPILOGUE

Night came. Ian felt a terrible ache as he wheeled toward the campfire circle, hearing the crackle of the flames. Whirling in his head were a million memories he'd gathered since first entering this circle.

The smell of burning wood was in the air, and smoke rose past the tall pines into the darkness as he found a place. Then Susanna wheeled over with a big smile on her face. The flickering orange flames reflected from her protective helmet as she handed Ian a slip of paper.

"This is my address," she said shyly. "I hope you'll write to me."

"Thanks, Susanna." Ian scribbled his own address for her. "Where's Blondie? I'd like to write her, too."

"She's not here, but I can tell you where to send a letter."

"Has she gone with her mom in the camp bus?"

"No, she's in Regina seeing her dad. Her parents split up recently."

"I didn't know that. She's always so cheerful."

Susanna smiled. "That's Blondie. The brightest ray of sunshine around."

They said goodbye, and Susanna wheeled away. Ian looked with deep affection at Linda and the others. Winn, who'd been the first to show him the meaning of courage ... Parrish, with whom he'd shared so much ... Greyeyes, Rico, Ken and Corny ... it was hard to believe that tomorrow they'd no longer be together.

The evening passed too quickly, but instead of feeling the pain of saying goodbye Ian was already anticipating the joy of returning to camp next summer. As the circle joined hands for a final song, and the firelight glistened on

faces wet with tears, Ian took Corny's hand.
Then, smiling, he also reached to Parrish. With a
glowing heart, he joined in the singing of words
that meant so much:

> Tell me why the stars do shine
> Tell me why the ivy twines
> Tell me why the sky's so blue
> Tell me, Camp Easter Seal, just why
>   I love you.

This picture shows Eric Wilson when he was a
counsellor at Camp Easter Seal. For more
information about Camp Easter Seal, write to:
    Saskatchewan Abilities Council
    1410 Kilburn Avenue
    Saskatoon, Saskatchewan
    S7M 0J8

    or to the Easter Seal Society
    in your province.